MR. WILMER

MR. WILMER

by ROBERT LAWSON

ILLUSTRATED BY THE AUTHOR

LITTLE, BROWN AND COMPANY · BOSTON

1946

Published May 1945
Reprinted May 1945
Reprinted September 1945
Reprinted November 1945
Reprinted March 1946

Contents

MR. WILMER

The most useless day of all is that in which we have not laughed.

— SÉBASTIEN R. N. CHAMFORT

Saturday's Child Has Far to Go

W ILLIAM WILMER was twenty-nine years old before he discovered that he could converse with animals. In fact it happened on his twenty-ninth birthday and it made a great difference in his life. From then on, life became highly exciting and lots of fun. He was always a little sorry that he hadn't discovered his great gift sooner, because up to that time existence had been very dull indeed. However, as Mrs. Keeler, his landlady, always said — especially when she looked at her husband — "You can't expect everything," so Mr. Wilmer was quite content with the way things worked out.

William Wilmer's twenty-ninth birthday (it came on the nineteenth of April) started just the same as any other day. In fact each of his days, except Sunday, started just the same as every other day, and ended about the same. He wouldn't have remembered that it *was* his birthday, except that in the morning he had received the usual greeting card from his Aunt Edna in Peoria — Aunt Edna never failed to send one. There was always a picture of a bunch of flowers printed on it and the words BIRTHDAY GREETINGS TO A DEAR NEPHEW. And written in purple ink there was always the same message: *You see I never forget, just like the elephant, ha! ha! Your loving* AUNT EDNA.

Sometimes Mr. Wilmer wished she *would* forget, just for a change; and having once seen a snapshot of Aunt Edna he thought the elephant simile was rather unwisely chosen. However, he dutifully removed last year's card from the mirror over his bureau and stuck up the new one, where it would remain until next birthday.

This morning, just as every other morning, Mr. Wilmer walked three blocks across town and three blocks down, to where there was a bus stop. It was a beautiful spring morning, quite warm for the nineteenth of April, as Mr. and Mrs. Keeler had both remarked — twice. There had been a shower during the night and now little wisps of steam were rising from the sidewalk wherever the sun struck. An ice wagon rattled by, the driver whistling loudly. A little bird of some sort hopped about in a starved-looking tree and whistled back at him. William Wilmer had a strange, vague feeling that something unusual was stirring in the air today, that today something *different*

was going to happen. It disturbed him a little, for he was so used to things being the same that the thought of any change was a bit frightening. "I guess it's just spring," he thought — and, recollecting the birthday card: "After all, twenty-nine isn't so *terribly* old."

The bus took him seven blocks crosstown and twelve down, to the subway station. At the newsstand there, just as every morning, he bought his copy of the *Daily Bleat* and a roll of Peppermint Patooties. On the subway train he sat in his regular front right-hand corner seat of the fourth car, took one Peppermint Patootie, and looked at the pictures of murderers, gunmen and politicians, as far as 72nd Street. At 72nd Street, as usual, he ate his second Patootie and turned to the comic page. There was always just time between 72nd Street and his stop to look at "Captain Super" and "Bring 'em Back Dead," fold the paper and put it in his pocket for Claude the elevator starter, straighten his hat and unwrap three Patooties for the Policeman's horse.

The Policeman always sat on his horse halfway up the first block from the subway station and for as many mornings as he could remember Mr. Wilmer had always stopped and given the horse three Peppermint Patooties. The horse had learned to recognize him (which few people ever did) and always pawed at the curb and stretched out his neck eagerly at his approach. It was the pleasantest thing in Mr. Wilmer's day; that and saying "Good morning" to that red-headed Miss Sweeney who sat four desks away from him at the office.

The Policeman had never appeared to notice Mr. Wilmer. He always sat up very straight, glaring at the traffic, but this morning he suddenly turned down a beefy, unpleasant face and growled, "Leave off feedin' the horse sugar."

Mr. Wilmer was stunned and quite terrified. It was the first time in his life that a Policeman had ever spoken to him. He could feel little prickles run up his spine, he burst into a sweat and his knees felt weak.

He was conscious of the horse's whiskers tickling his hand, of the warm breath that was making the Patooties soft and sticky. Hastily he snatched back the offending offering and tried to speak, but his voice was husky and not very steady.

"Excuse me," he stammered, "I didn't know. It's — er — they're not really sugar. They're peppermint — er — Peppermint Patooties."

The Policeman had resumed his statuelike pose and was again glaring at the traffic. Without even bothering to look down he rumbled, "Peppermint or spearmint or potaties or patooties or sugar or salt — leave off feedin' the horse, that's all."

Burning with embarrassment William Wilmer stumbled away. His head was buzzing, his hand was stuck up with Peppermint Patooties, but he dared not throw them in the gutter — he remembered the signs: Do Not Litter Your Streets. He tried to put them in his pocket, but they only gathered tufts of fuzz and stuck tighter.

As he hastened from the scene of his humiliation he suddenly heard a voice speaking. It was a small voice, very small and far away, but perfectly clear and distinct. "The big, bullnecked, ham-faced, overbearing bully," it was saying, "the stupid, selfish, heavy-bottomed brute! I'll get even with him, I'll fix him — "

Mr. Wilmer glanced back over his shoulder and was astonished to discover that there was no one anywhere near. There were only the Policeman, his red neck bulging over his collar, and the impatiently pawing horse. "That's queer," he thought, but he was so confused and upset that he did not realize how queer it really was.

He hurried into the lobby of the Safe, Sane and Colossal Insurance Company Building, forgot to give Claude the starter his copy of the *Daily Bleat*, and was rewarded for his thoughtlessness by having the elevator door slammed on his heel.

Ever since he had finished High School eleven years ago, William Wilmer had worked for the Safe, Sane and Colossal Insurance Company. The office where he spent his days was on the ninth floor of the S. S. & C. Building. It was a huge room, almost a block square and filled with rows of desks, very much like a schoolroom. There were seventeen aisles and six desks in each row between the aisles. Mr. Wilmer's desk was in the seventh row, second from the left of Aisle J. On each desk was either a typewriter or a calculating machine. Mr. Wilmer's desk had a calculator.

At night the machines were protected by covers of rubberized cloth and every morning punctually at 8:57 William Wilmer sat down at his desk, took off the cover, folded it neatly and placed it in the lower right-hand drawer of his desk. Then he pulled up his cuffs, eased his coat and started to work.

On the right-hand corner of his desk there was always waiting a square wire basket filled with long slips of pink, green or yellow paper on which were columns of figures. The figures on the pink slips were to be added, those on the green slips to be divided and the yellow ones subtracted. So all day Mr. Wilmer punched at the keys of his machine, adding, subtracting or dividing. The results came out on strips of white paper which he carefully placed in a wire basket on the *left*-hand corner of his desk. Punctually, every hour, an office boy brought a fresh basketful of pink, green and yellow slips and carried away the white ones. At 4:57 each afternoon a buzzer sounded, Mr. Wilmer pulled down his cuffs and coat sleeves, put the cover on his machine and went home.

It was not a very exciting life.

The only exciting thing was when he smiled good morning to that redheaded Miss Sweeney who sat four desks to the right of him across Aisle J. Her hair, although undeniably red, was soft and wavy. It looked as though it had been brushed a great deal, not just kinked up with cheap permanents like that of most of the other girls. Her eyes were deep blue, with black-lashed rims, and when she smiled her nose, which was extremely short, wrinkled in a most entrancing way. Her morning greeting made William Wilmer feel warm and happy for hours. He could punch cheerily at the keys of his machine and forget

all about the Safe, Sane and Colossal Insurance Company and Mrs. Keeler's tiresome boardinghouse. He didn't quite know just what he *did* think about at those times, but they were very pleasant thoughts.

This morning however, his birthday morning, everything was wrong. He was still red and confused from the Policeman's rudeness. He removed the cover from his machine, placed it in the lower right-hand drawer, pulled up his cuffs, eased his coat and looked over to smile good morning to Miss Sweeney. She wasn't there.

He guessed at once that she was in one of the inner offices taking dictation and he was right, for soon she emerged from Mr. Twitch's office looking extremely angry, slammed her notebook on her desk and began hammering furiously at her typewriter without even glancing in Mr. Wilmer's direction.

"Oh well," he sighed, "I might have known it — everything's wrong this morning." He did not have to wonder why Miss Sweeney was mad; everyone who had any dealings with Mr. Twitch always came away angry.

Mr. A. Wellington Twitch was the Office Manager and was a thoroughly unpleasant creature. He wasn't much older than Mr. Wilmer, but he *looked* much older, for he was slightly bald and was becoming stout, a fact which he tried to conceal by always wearing tightly buttoned double-breasted coats. His neckties

always matched his socks and the neatly pressed handkerchief which peeped from his breast pocket always
matched the necktie. This handkerchief was only for
show; the one he really used was carried in his trousers-
pocket and was generally damp and not too clean, for
Mr. Twitch usually had a cold in the head.

His full name was Arthur Wellington Twitch and
it is conceivable, though not likely, that when he was
young his mother called him Artie or his playmates
called him "Art," but it seemed impossible now that
he could have ever been called anything so affection-
ate. It seemed still more impossible that he could ever
have had any playmates.

William Wilmer was still thinking about what an
unhappy morning it had been when he became aware
that Mr. Twitch was standing beside his desk. He was
twisting his little black mustache, a sure sign that he
was preparing to be particularly nasty, and speaking
in a loud voice so that everyone around could hear.

"Well, Wilmer," he was saying, "daydreaming
again, I see. It's really a shame that our little duties
here should interfere with your slumbers. Perhaps
they will not — very much longer. Three mistakes
this morning — three: two additions and one subtraction and in the amount of three dollars, eighty-seven
cents."

Mr. Wilmer, hot and confused, tried to stammer
something about being sorry, but Mr. Twitch was en-

joying himself now and went on in a louder and more sneering tone.

"Of course, to a man of your financial standing the sum of three dollars, eighty-seven cents is practically nothing, a mere bagatelle, as it were, but I can assure you that the Safe, Sane and Colossal Insurance Company, Incorporated, does not share your views. Nor does the Safe, Sane and Colossal Company appreciate your innovations in the science of addition and subtraction; and what's more they're not going to put up with it. Now watch your step, my lad. One more mistake like this — just one — and you'll be out in the street. And I can tell you, jobs don't grow on trees these days."

As he strutted off one or two of the clerks tittered, but Miss Sweeney did not. She looked more angry than ever and it was some consolation to William Wilmer to see her nose wrinkle with distaste and the small tip of a very pink tongue protrude slightly at the retreating back of A. Wellington Twitch.

She gave Mr. Wilmer a sweet and sympathetic smile, but he was too miserable now to be cheered by anything. It certainly was being a happy birthday! All he could do was to keep punching at the keys of his machine and wait for the noontime buzzer to buzz. He made several mistakes, but didn't know and didn't care.

This morning, it being Saturday, the office closed at noon. At 11:57 the office boys went up and down the aisles placing small envelopes on all the desks. William Wilmer put his in his pocket without even opening it. It was his weekly wage and he knew that it contained exactly $34.86, less Social Security, bond payments, Withholding Tax and so on.

As he emerged from the S. S. & C. Building he noticed that it was much warmer. Spring had really arrived and this made him feel even more depressed. He didn't care much for Saturday afternoons at any time, but in spring and summer he liked them even less. Everyone was always hurrying toward the stations and the ferries and the bus terminals. They were laden with bags, picnic baskets, tennis rackets, golf clubs, bathing suits and kodaks. He knew they were going to the beaches or to the country for week ends, but he didn't know anyone who would invite him to the country for a week end and he didn't care much for the beaches, he always got pushed around so much — besides, he sunburned very easily.

So he usually went to a movie on Saturday afternoon and to another one Saturday evening. Sundays were different, they were all right. Because then there were the Sunday papers to read and William Wilmer read every one of them from beginning to end. He read the news and the editorials, the scientific articles and the book reviews. He read the real estate advertisements, the Garden Section, the society notes and even the recipes and the funnies. But what he enjoyed most of all were the Vacation Travel Sections; he read every word of those. He read about cruises to the Caribbean and Nova Scotia and Labrador and Alaska. And about the Grand Canyon and Yellowstone Park, where you could feed the bears; about California and Florida. He liked to picture himself clad in immaculate white linens, stretched in a deck chair, while the ship plowed gently through soft tropical seas and the Southern Cross glowed warmly above the horizon.

Somehow in these imaginings that redheaded Miss Sweeney was always there too. He could picture just how well she would wear Southern resort clothes (he even picked out several outfits for her from the better

advertisements) and how her coppery hair would seem
even more burnished under a Southern sun and how
her very short nose would wrinkle even more fas-
cinatingly as she gazed with delight on the beauties
of strange far places. Yes, Sundays were all right.

And then Sunday afternoons he always went over
to the Zoo and looked at the animals. He didn't know
much about animals, but he liked them. They were so
powerful and lithe, yet so resigned to being shut up
in cages. Somehow he felt a great kinship with them,
for after all, his life in the Safe, Sane and Colossal Insurance Company office was pretty much the same as
theirs. Only *they* didn't have any Mr. A. Wellington
Twitch to boss them around. He was sure that none
of the Zoo's keepers would ever dare be as mean as
Mr. Twitch — some tiger or puma would have his leg
off in a minute.

What with the spring and the warmth and the unpleasant events of the morning Mr. Wilmer was completely upset and out of sorts. Suddenly, with reckless self-abandon, he decided, "I think I'll go to the
Zoo this afternoon instead of tomorrow." It was quite
a grave change from the routine of eleven years of
established habit, but he felt really desperate. Perhaps
the quiet companionship of the animals would help re-
store his nerves, so without giving himself time to
change his mind he hastily boarded a bus and went
up to the Zoo.

There were fewer people about than he had expected. The sudden warm weather had made the animal houses seem unbearably stuffy and most people were sprawled on the lawns or messing around on the ponds. William Wilmer wandered through the Large Mammal House and paused in front of his favorite cage. The sign on it said AFRICAN LION (*Felis leo*) — and another sign said TOBY. Toby was Mr. Wilmer's favorite, for of all the animals he seemed the handsomest and most resigned. All day he lay with his proud yellow eyes staring fixedly into space, contemptuous alike of old ladies' poking umbrellas or children's tossed candies.

Today, however, he was restless. He paced and tossed and shook his head. He flopped down and stretched his legs, clawed at the floor and rose and paced again.

Mr. Wilmer hadn't noticed. He was still too upset to notice anything much. He kept seeing the Policeman's angry red face, he remembered the sticky Peppermint Patooties clasped in his hand. He could see Mr. Twitch twisting his little black mustache and hear his sarcastic, rasping voice.

He remembered, too, that other voice, that small faraway one that he had heard in the street when there was no one there but the Policeman and his horse. It was queer, that was; he couldn't imagine what it could have been.

And then he suddenly heard it again! It was the same voice or one very much like it, small and far away, but perfectly clear and distinct. It was saying, "Well, what have *you* got to be grumbling about?"

William Wilmer looked around to see who was talking, but for once, the Lion House was completely empty of people. There was no one at all, except himself and one Keeper, who was way down at the other end, sweeping and whistling softly; it couldn't be he. Astonished, he looked all around again and then noticed Toby's yellow eyes fixed intently on his face. At last it began to dawn on him that it was Toby speaking — speaking to him, and rather irritably. The great lips scarcely moved, the voice seemed to come from somewhere way inside. It seemed very small for a lion, but perfectly clear.

"Well," said Toby, "I asked, 'What have *you* to be grumbling about?' "

Mr. Wilmer didn't know quite how to answer. He knew Toby could not understand him if he just spoke in his ordinary voice. It ought to be that small faraway sound; far away and small, but clear and distinct. He tried very hard, he did funny little things with the muscles of his throat and suddenly it came! It came from somewhere way down deep, he didn't have to do anything with his lips or tongue, it just came out, small and far away, very much like Toby's or the Policeman's horse's, but a little thinner.

"Why I wasn't — er — grumbling — exactly," said William Wilmer with his new voice. "I was just sort of thinking and talking to myself, I guess. You see, it's been a very upsetting day. There was that unpleasant Policeman and Mr. Twitch — it was mostly Twitch I think that got me worked up — "

"Twitch," snorted Toby, "Twitch — what's a twitch to bother anybody? Young man, did you ever have a *twinge?*" He hitched himself closer to the bars. "Did you ever have a *pain?* A searing, blinding, red-

hot spasm burning through your jaw and down the side of your neck like a bolt of slow lightning?" He hitched himself still closer. "Young man, did you ever have a TOOTHACHE?"

"Oh, yes indeed," said William sympathetically. "When I was in High School once I had a dreadful time. It was a wisdom tooth — infected — it was really terrible. I know how you must feel."

"You do *not*," answered Toby. "You can't have the faintest conception." He sniffed tolerantly and opened his mouth wide to show the rows of great glistening fangs. " 'Terrible'!" he snorted. "What would *you* know about terrible, with those tiny little chips of teeth you have? Why this single one of mine, upper right eyetooth — that's the one that's giving me the agony — why that one tooth has more ivory in it than you have in your whole head, and that much more pain too.

"And the trouble is — " he banged the bars irritably — "the trouble is that these blithering idiots can't find out what's the matter with me."

"Why don't you tell them?" asked Mr. Wilmer. "Why don't you tell them, like you've just told me?"

"Tell them?" snapped Toby. "Don't you think I would if I could? It just happens that you're the first and only human I've seen since I was brought to this God-forsaken, dreary country who could understand Animal or speak Animal, the very first. Now if you would only tell them for me — " A fresh spasm of pain caused him to emit a series of heartrending roars.

Mr. Wilmer, politely waiting for the pain to pass, was suddenly conscious of the Keeper at his side.

"Now then, now then," said the Keeper. "Don't be bothering the animal. It's bad enough he is, let alone, what with something ailing him and nobody knowing what. Four days and nights he's been roaring and bellering and me not able to do anything for him, not even clean the cage, that ugly-tempered he is, and him that's usually a lamb."

"It's a toothache," said Mr. Wilmer. "The upper right eyetooth."

The Keeper regarded him severely. "Toothache is it?" he inquired. "Toothache you say — and in the upper right eyetooth? And just what might *you* be, to be telling *me* about his toothaches and eyeteeth? A mind reader perhaps, or maybe one of them Indian physics or swamis? Here's the Director been up with him two nights, and the State Veterinary, and him with his stethoscopes and X-rays and injections and all, and devil a thing can they find ailing poor Toby — and you to be telling me it's the toothache!"

"I'm sure it is," said Mr. Wilmer. "He just told me so. He said — "

"He *what?*" asked the Keeper slowly.

"He *said* it was the toothache — the upper right eyetooth. You see, we were talking about toothaches and how painful they can be and he said — "

The Keeper grasped Mr. Wilmer kindly, but firmly, by the elbow and started walking him toward the door, talking all the while in a soothing tone.

"Sure and it's a *very* hot day, unseasonable really and the sun real strong for this time in April. You wouldn't have been walking without your hat would you, or maybe have a drop of liquor under your belt, or two perhaps, it being Saturday afternoon and all? We'll just be stepping out into the good fresh air now, quiet like and not making any disturbances — disturbances disturbs the animals, especially in this spring weather." They were outside now and the Keeper steered Mr. Wilmer toward a shady path. "Right down by the lake there," he said, "there'll be plenty of benches, cool and in the shade — sitting there awhile you'll likely feel better."

He went back toward the Lion House shaking his head. "Too bad," he said. "A nice lad he seemed, quiet and well-behaved. He didn't *look* nuts. It just goes to show — you never can tell."

William Wilmer did sit in the shade for a while and tried to collect his thoughts, but it was rather difficult. It had been a most confusing day and he felt very tired. He decided to go home to Mrs. Keeler's and retire right after dinner, he certainly didn't want to go to any movie. He felt as though he *were* a movie, a sort of one-man two-reel comedy.

The Day of Rest

~~~~~~~~~~ S ~~~~~~~~~~

UNDAY MORNING
Mr. Wilmer woke quite early. The soft breeze stirring
his window curtains promised a day still warmer than
yesterday, the air even *smelled* springlike. He decided
to walk to the corner and get the Sunday papers before breakfast instead of afterward as he usually did.
"My, I certainly am becoming unpredictable," he
thought.

As he went down Mrs. Keeler's front steps it was
almost like walking into a greenhouse, the morning
was so balmy. Down the street two whitewings were
flushing the pavement with a fire hose and whenever
the stream splashed up from the curbing the early
sun struck sparkles and rainbows in the dancing spray.
The water ran clear and bubbling down the gutters
with little brooklike gurglings.

The same feeling of something impending that had

come over him yesterday morning was even stronger today. Certainly, plenty had happened yesterday, mostly unpleasant, but that business of hearing the Policeman's horse and talking with Toby had been very pleasant and most exciting, although quite mystifying. It seemed so long ago he wondered if all those things actually could have happened; it didn't seem possible, he must have imagined everything. Perhaps the Keeper at the Zoo *had* been right, it might have been the heat, or something he had eaten. Yet he could still hear those small, clear voices, he could remember exactly how he had done something queer with the muscles way down in his throat and how, without his even moving his lips or tongue, his own small, clear Animal voice had come out, perfectly distinct and understandable to Toby, although apparently inaudible to anyone else.

There was a milk wagon standing beside the curb. The big, dappled gray horse looked tired, his head hung sleepily. On a sudden impulse Mr. Wilmer decided to try out his new voice. He didn't see the driver anywhere, but he carefully clasped his hands behind his back; no use being called down again for feeding someone's horse.

Then William Wilmer did those strange little things with his throat muscles and the small, clear voice came out just as it had done yesterday. "Good morning," he said politely, "quite warm, isn't it?"

The horse opened one eye, fixing it wearily on Mr. Wilmer, and *his* voice came, much like Toby's but even more like the Policeman's horse's. "Morning," he grunted. "Got the time?"

Mr. Wilmer consulted his watch and announced that it was about 7:45.

"Half an hour more," said the horse, closing his eye again. "The rest of this block — down the Avenue — all the next block — down the Avenue — then back to the stables." He suddenly opened both eyes and stared sorrowfully at Mr. Wilmer. "Ever do any night work, young feller?" Without waiting for a reply, he snorted, "Well, don't!" and closed his eyes again.

The rattling of bottles announced the approach of the driver, and automatically, head hanging and eyes still closed, the old horse clopped along to the next building.

William Wilmer, standing in the deserted street, was swept by a great wave of elation and excitement. It *was* true! He *could* actually talk with animals!

He hurried home with the papers, his mind in a dazed whirl. This accomplishment promised to make life much more interesting; week ends would no longer be boring. . . . He didn't dream *how* interesting life was going to be.

At breakfast Mrs. Keeler inquired: "In early, weren't you? No movie?"

"No," answered Mr. Wilmer, "I was sort of tired, it was quite hot yesterday, and I just didn't feel like it."

Mr. Keeler, helping himself to a third cup of coffee, winked heavily. "Spring," he pronounced. "Ah, spring! In spring a young man's fancy — "

Mrs. Keeler quenched him with a glance. "You're not a young man," she said, "and Heaven knows you're not fancy — and as for spring, there's that bedspring in the third floor front you're to fix today, I'm glad you reminded me of it."

"Yes, my dear," said Mr. Keeler, wiping his walrus mustache with a loud swishing noise. "I was considering that, just as soon as I have glanced at the headlines." He picked up Mr. Wilmer's Sunday papers.

"Ah, here's an interesting item — 'Zoo's Prize Lion Suffering from Mysterious Ailment.'"

"Give Mr. Wilmer his own paper," Mrs. Keeler interrupted, "and get going."

Mr. Wilmer glanced at the front page and there, staring out with his patient eyes, was a large photograph of Toby. He began to read the article aloud: "Officials of the Central Zoo have been greatly concerned by the inexplicable illness of Toby, the Zoo's oldest and most prized lion. Dr. Wimpole, State Veterinary, has made several examinations and taken numerous blood tests without any result. X-ray photographs have failed to reveal the seat of the trouble. Carrington Carrington-Carr, Director of the Central Zoo, confesses himself completely baffled. Three eminent specialists, summoned last week from Johns Hopkins, recommended a diet of Vitamins A, E, I, O, U and sometimes Y, but the patient has shown no improvement. A further consultation of experts will take place this morning — "

"Why, that's silly!" Mr. Wilmer broke off. "It's only a toothache, upper right eyetooth; why, just yesterday he said — "

He became aware that both Mr. and Mrs. Keeler were eying him oddly. "And how," Mrs. Keeler inquired quietly, "and how would *you* know it was toothache — and upper right eyetooth at that — and *who* was it said just what?"

"Why, Toby," he began. "He said — " Then suddenly Mr. Wilmer remembered the Keeper at the Zoo yesterday. He remembered the queer way the Keeper had eyed him as he led him from the Lion House, and now saw that same queer look pass between Mr. and Mrs. Keeler.

"I — ah — don't remember," he stammered, hurriedly. "Do you know, I think I'll walk over to the Zoo this morning" — and he hastily retreated from the dining room.

Mrs. Keeler was lost in speculation as the front door closed. "Funny," she mused. "No movie last night and he always goes Saturdays, out for the papers before breakfast and he never does that, to the Zoo this morning and he always goes in the afternoon — "

"Spring, my dear," said Mr. Keeler, rummaging for the sporting page. "Spring — birds — flowers — Love, maybe."

"Love . . ." said Mrs. Keeler picking up the coffee pot and balancing it thoughtfully, as a discus thrower weighs his missile. "Spring . . . Spring, my love — and spring fast. Bedspring — third-floor front."

Mr. Keeler sprang.

As Mr. Wilmer entered the Park he heard a sound that seemed like distant thunder, but the sky was unusually blue and the sun shone warmly. "Must be building a new subway," he thought. As he neared the Lion House, however, he realized that the sound was the roaring of animals. All the lions and tigers, the leopards, panthers and pumas seemed to be holding forth at a great rate, but one set of roars was much louder and more thunderous than all the others. "Goodness, what a noise," said Mr. Wilmer, as he entered the building. It was empty of people, for the morning was still early.

He went straight to Toby's cage, only to find the bars covered by a large canvas sheet on which was hung a sign, CLOSED FOR REPAIRS. The loudest roars were coming from this cage, and between the roars Mr. Wilmer could hear men's voices and the shuffling of feet.

As he stood there two men came hurrying by. One was the Keeper who had escorted him out the day before, the other was a tall worried-looking man dressed in rough gray tweeds. The Keeper spied Mr. Wilmer, paused, and then suddenly pounced on him with a glad cry.

"This is him," he shouted, above the roaring of the animals. "This is him, Mr. Carrington-Carr, this is the guy!"

The tall man removed an unlighted pipe from his mouth and inquired, "What guy, Gallagher?"

"The one I was after telling you about," cried the Keeper excitedly. "Him that said to me yesterday 'twas the toothache was bothering poor Toby; upper

right eyetooth he said, didn't you now?" He shook Mr. Wilmer's arm. "Didn't you say 'twas the toothache?"

"Why yes, I did," answered Mr. Wilmer, slightly dazed by the noise and the Keeper's excitement.

The tall man extended his hand and smiled pleasantly. "My name is Carrington-Carr," he said. "Carrington Carrington-Carr, Director here. Keeper Gallagher has told us a rather odd story of your visit here yesterday and of your truly extraordinary diagnosis of Toby's trouble. Tell me now, just what was it led you to believe that it was toothache?"

Mr. Wilmer hesitated, he didn't want *everyone* to

think he was crazy; but this man seemed pleasant and intelligent — perhaps he would understand. "Well — you see," he stammered, "he — er — that is — Toby *said* so. We were just sort of talking about things and he said that he had a terrible toothache, upper right eyetooth, and he said — I'm sorry, but his own words were: 'These blithering idiots can't find out what's the matter with me.'"

Mr. Carrington-Carr flashed a startled glance at the Keeper, but went on quietly. "If Toby possesses this remarkable linguistic ability, which we have certainly never noted, why do you suppose he didn't tell *us* his troubles?"

"Why — er — he said that I was the first person he had met who could understand Animal or talk Animal."

"Have you been aware of this great gift long?" the Director asked.

"No sir, I only discovered it yesterday," Mr. Wilmer answered. "It was a great surprise, I can assure you."

"I don't doubt that," said Mr. Carrington-Carr with a slight smile. "Tell me now, just how *does* one converse with an animal? Let us suppose, for a moment, that I am a lion; would you mind just saying 'Good morning' to me?"

"Certainly not," said William Wilmer. He did the strange little things with his throat muscles and heard his small, faraway, clear voice say, "Good morning, Mr. Carrington-Carr, nice day."

"Well, go ahead," said the Director.

"I have — I did," Mr. Wilmer answered. "I said 'Good morning, Mr. Carrington-Carr.'"

Again the Director exchanged glances with the Keeper. "I didn't hear anything, did you, Gallagher?"

"Devil a word," he answered. "I told you he was nuts."

"Perhaps if you really *were* a lion — " began Mr. Wilmer.

"Don't get fresh with the Director — " interrupted Gallagher, but Mr. Carrington-Carr silenced him.

"Nuts or not," he said, "or voices or no voices, the fact still remains that none of our precious experts had been able to discover what Toby's trouble was until at our consultation last night you mentioned this young man's seemingly fantastic story. As you remember, more in desperation than anything else, we took new X-rays of Toby's teeth, and discovered that the diagnosis was absolutely correct. It *is* toothache, and as far as we can tell, it *is* the upper right eyetooth, although we are not absolutely certain on this latter point.

"Come, let's find out," he ended suddenly and led the way through an office and into a narrow brick passage that ran back of the cages. It was a very narrow passage and they had to pass much too close to the bars for William Wilmer's comfort, for all the animals, excited by Toby's roars, were also roaring and pacing their cages excitedly. In the passage, back of Toby's cage, was a group of young men, many of whom carried cameras while the rest had note-books. Mr. Wilmer judged they were newspaper reporters.

"Stand aside, boys, and leave the Director get by," shouted Mr. Gallagher; "and mind now, none of your flashlights till you get permission, the poor beast is excited enough as it is."

In the cage were several distinguished-looking gen-tlemen, most of them in surgeons' white coats. There were two Keepers, armed with heavy iron bars, and a table covered with a white cloth on which was spread an array of shiny surgical instruments. The sight of these made Mr. Wilmer feel somewhat sick-ish, so he turned his attention to the patient.

Poor Toby looked far from dignified or resigned. He was spread-eagled out on the floor; heavy ropes stretched from his paws to the four corners of the cage. A thick piece of wood was stuck between his jaws and lashed tightly with stout cords, but he man-aged to keep up a continual roaring and moaning in spite of the gag.

"Gentlemen," said Director Carrington-Carr, rais-ing his hand for attention, "allow me to present Mr. — er — "

"Wilmer," said Mr. Wilmer, "William Wilmer."

"Gentlemen," went on the Director, "Mr. Wilmer is the young man whose uncannily accurate diagnosis enabled us to locate the seat of Toby's trouble. You will, of course, recollect Keeper Gallagher's extraordinary tale at our consultation last evening.

"Mr. Wilmer, it seems, by his own account, was enabled to accomplish this remarkable diagnosis by conversing with Toby in a private form of language with which very few humans are privileged to be conversant. In short, he talked to the lion and the lion told him what the trouble was."

At this a chorus of talk and laughter arose from the newsmen and even the dignified gentlemen in white coats smiled broadly.

"Pipe down, youse," Mr. Gallagher warned the reporters as he toyed with his iron bar, "or out you go."

Mr. Carrington-Carr motioned the scientists closer and continued: "We have not time, at the moment, to go into this remarkable phenomenon, if it is; that can come later. The important thing is that this young man's diagnosis has been, thus far, absolutely correct, as proven by our X-rays. He also says that the trouble is with the upper right eyetooth. Of this we have no proof and to pull the wrong tooth of an animal as valuable as this would be an extremely grave error. I therefore propose to allow Mr. Wilmer to converse quietly with Toby for a few moments and make as certain as is humanly possible that we are doing the right thing. It may help us and it certainly cannot do any harm."

William Wilmer knelt down and put his hand on Toby's feverish paw. He did the peculiar things with his throat muscles and heard his small, faraway voice say, "Well, Toby, they certainly have got you down."

Toby answered, *his* small voice much muffled by the gag, "How han I hawk wiv his ham hick in my mou?"

Mr. Wilmer looked up at the small ring of intent faces. "He says he can't talk well with that stick in his mouth. Could you take it out?"

Mr. Gallagher and another Keeper gingerly untied the lashings and Toby disgustedly spat out the heavy stick. "There, that's *less* bad," he grumbled. "*Now* what is it?"

Mr. Wilmer said, "Toby, these gentlemen have at last found out what your trouble is and they want to relieve it as quickly as possible, only they're not absolutely certain which tooth it is."

"I *told* you," Toby answered irritably. "I told you it was the upper right eyetooth; why didn't you tell *them?*"

"I tried to," apologized Mr. Wilmer, "I *did* try to, but they all thought I was crazy. Perhaps I'd better point it out to them, so there can't be any mistake. This is the one, isn't it?" And he placed his finger on the great gleaming fang. Toby emitted a roar that shook the building and brought down a small snowstorm of flaked paint from the ceiling.

"I guess that's the one all right," said Mr. Wilmer, turning to the Director and the attentive scientists.

They went to work at once. The stick was replaced and well tied. Two white-coated doctors shot huge syringes of anesthetic into Toby's gums; then, while the keepers held his head firmly, another doctor clamped a shiny pair of forceps on the upper right eyetooth. He struggled and wrestled and yanked while Toby's roars made the canvas screen flap as though in a summer wind. Finally, with a great heave

and a piercing bellow, the tooth came out, followed
by a rush of blood. Other doctors hastily closed in
and examined the cavity with flashlights and magni-
fying glasses.

"He's right!" they chorused excitedly. "That *is* the
one — badly ulcerated too!"

The exhausted doctor who had done the pulling
advanced with the gory fang still clamped in his
forceps. "Here it is, Mr. Wilmer," he cried. "That's
the baby, you had it right."

But Mr. Wilmer wasn't there. At the first gush of
blood he had quietly fainted and now lay flat on the
floor, his head under the instrument table.

When he came to, he was in the Director's office. His hair was wet and his collar sopping, for Keeper Gallagher had helpfully tossed a bucket of water over him. His head was buzzing and his eyes dazzled by the continuous popping of flashlights. His nostrils were filled with the fumes of smelling salts and his ears with the shouts of the reporters and photographers: "Give us a smile now, Bud." "Look over here, attaboy." "What's your address?" "Where do you work?" "How's about a smile?" "When did you learn to talk the lingo?" "Married?" "Got a girl friend?"

William Wilmer answered their questions as well as he could, which wasn't very well, for he still felt dizzy and the flashlights made his head ache.

"How's about a few pictures with the animal?" asked one of the photographers, so they all trooped back to the cage. The ropes that held poor Toby had been eased so that he could lie more comfortably.

"Do you feel better?" Mr. Wilmer inquired anxiously.

"Ever so much better," replied Toby. "Pain's all gone. Jaw's sore though, probably have to eat mush and trash for a few days. I'm certainly grateful to you though."

"Don't mention it," Mr. Wilmer answered. "Sorry I couldn't have helped you sooner."

They took pictures of Mr. Wilmer sitting with his arm around Toby's neck, of Mr. Wilmer patting

Toby, of Mr. Wilmer shaking hands with the Director, with the Keeper and with each of the scientific gentlemen.

"Come on, Daniel," called one of the photographers. "Let's have one with your hand in the lion's mouth." So Mr. Wilmer obligingly posed with his hand in Toby's mouth while Toby smiled pleasantly. However, when they demanded that he pose holding up the tooth, he began to turn green again and the Director called a halt.

They had lunch in the Director's office. It was a large, pleasant room looking out through the trees to the lake and it was a very good lunch too, but Mr.

Wilmer didn't get a chance to eat much of it, for the scientists kept plying him with questions. Every time he tried to swallow anything one of them would place a stethoscope against his throat and listen. They listened to his head and his back and his chest, they shined flashlights in his eyes and looked in his ears through little silver funnels.

Each of them wanted William Wilmer to visit him in order to undergo more thorough investigation; and before the luncheon was over he had promised to go to Chicago, Boston, Battle Creek, Washington and Baltimore. He hadn't any idea of just how or when he could go, but the gentlemen were all so pleasant and eager that he couldn't refuse.

After lunch Director Carrington-Carr made a short speech.

"Gentlemen," he said, "we have today witnessed a most remarkable demonstration of something — we do not quite know what. Mr. Wilmer's belief in his ability to converse with animals is, I am sure, completely honest and sincere, and certainly seems to have been borne out by results in the case of Toby. However, as men of science it is, of course, our duty to be skeptical of *anything* new until it has been proved beyond the possibility of a doubt.

"I believe I have thought of a method by which we can test absolutely this gift of Mr. Wilmer's. I have here," and he held up a large ledger, "a complete life history of every animal in the Central Zoo; its age, birthplace, family tree, place of capture, date of arrival here, number of offspring, illnesses, operations and so on. This record is kept in my office safe and its contents are known only to me. It would seem a very simple matter to prove beyond all question this ability of our young friend, if we were to stroll about the grounds and allow him to interview various of the animals. If he can extract from them a few essential details of their private lives and if those details agree with our records, I can see no reason for doubting that he possesses some secret method, hitherto unknown to science, of communicating with the members of the animal kingdom. That is, of course, if Mr. Wilmer is willing to co-operate in this experiment."

"I'd be very glad to," said William Wilmer, struggling with a chocolate éclair, "very glad indeed."

It was quite an imposing group which set forth, all except Mr. Wilmer. His hair was still damp and stringy, his hat had been lost somewhere, and his collar was much the worse for wear. On his left walked Director Carrington-Carr and on his right Keeper Gallagher, carrying the official ledger. Behind them came the scientific gentlemen, in top hats and long coats, flanked by two guards to protect them from the crowd of newsmen and photographers. A great many small boys joined the procession, and sev-

eral dogs and three nursemaids pushing baby carriages. A balloon seller and a peanut vender with his push-cart brought up the rear.

"We might try Lucy first," said Mr. Carrington-Carr. "Here she is, right here." Lucy was an Indian elephant. She eyed the group with pleasant interest and extended her trunk for peanuts. Keeper Gallagher fumbled in his pocket for peanuts with one hand while he tried to open the ledger with the other.

"Now, Mr. Wilmer," said the Director, as the scientific gentlemen gathered close and the guards shoved the crowd back, "suppose you just ask Lucy a few questions: date of birth, place of capture, date of arrival here — just a few. Take your time and don't be nervous."

"None of them flashlights now," Mr. Gallagher cautioned.

Mr. Wilmer *was* nervous, though; he couldn't help being. He had never spoken with an elephant before,

and Lucy, although not especially large as elephants go, did loom up pretty imposingly.

He cleared his throat, did those funny little things with the muscles and in his small Animal voice said, "Good afternoon Miss Lucy, pleasant day isn't it?"

Lucy dropped Mr. Gallagher's peanuts, cocked up one ear and fixed her small twinkling eye on Mr. Wilmer. "Well, goodness gracious me!" she cried. "It certainly is pleasant to talk to someone; why, this is the first chance I've had since I left Burma, out there of course all the gentlemen know how to talk to us, even the little children do, and if there's one thing I love more than another it's talk. My, my, this *is* a pleasure. What did you say the name was?" — and extended her trunk.

"Wilmer," he answered, grasping the trunk cordially, "William Wilmer. You see," he went on hastily, for Lucy threatened to start chatting again, "I only discovered yesterday that I could talk with you people or I should have called on you sooner. But these gentlemen, Mr. Carrington-Carr, you're acquainted with him I suppose, and these scientists, don't quite believe I can do it — I can't quite believe it myself — and you could help me very much if you wouldn't mind answering a few questions."

"Not at all," replied Lucy pleasantly. "Delighted, I'm sure."

Mr. Wilmer looked at the Director. "What first?" he asked.

"Age," answered Carrington-Carr.

"Oh dear, I don't think I'd better ask that," Mr. Wilmer hesitated. "You see she's a lady. Perhaps we'd better start with birthplace. Where were you born, Miss Lucy?"

Lucy closed her eyes and recited, "I was born in the jungle of northeast Burma, about twelve miles north of the village of Bding Bdang. The village is not far from the border of Assam."

Mr. Wilmer repeated this information to the Director, who was intently studying the ledger. He looked startled, but merely said, "Go on — date of capture."

"When were you captured, Miss Lucy?" inquired Mr. Wilmer.

"Well, 'captured' is hardly the word," Lucy replied with a sigh, "I was captivated, really. It was an extremely handsome elephant in the herd of one Dhingbat Dhong, a resident of the village. I just sort of wandered in and joined the herd. I was young and inexperienced, of course, scarcely forty-eight at the time. That was back in 1915 — spring, naturally."

Mr. Wilmer relayed these facts to the Director, who looked still more startled. "Good Lord!" he murmured. "Go on — date of arrival at Zoo."

Mr. Wilmer was startled too, for glancing over Mr. Gallagher's shoulder he had caught a glimpse of these old entries in the ledger: —

BIRTHPLACE: Jungle of N. E. Burma.
PLACE OF CAPTURE: Bding Bdang.
DATE OF CAPTURE: April, 1915.
OWNER: Dhingbat Dhong.

"When did you arrive here at the Zoo, Miss Lucy?" he inquired.

Again she closed her eyes and thought back. "March 27, 1921, and a horrider day I've never known: rain, sleet and a chill that went through my bones like ice-water. I thought then, 'What a nasty climate this is,' and I've never thought any differently. Don't you think it's a nasty climate, Mr. Wilmer?"

"Indeed I do," he agreed. "Terrible." The next question was "Any offspring?" but he decided to skip that one too; after all, he had been calling her "Miss."

"Have you had any illnesses or operations since being here, Miss Lucy?" he asked instead.

"Nothing but head colds," she replied. "I have

those a great deal and you can't imagine how trying they can be with a nose the size of mine — not that it's unduly large, but still, five or six feet of nose is *something* when you have a cold in the head. The only serious thing was an infected toe. It was operated on a year ago last January, the sixteenth, I think. Dr. Wimpole did it, very skillful and a charming gentleman, but quite uneducated; I couldn't understand a word he said."

Mr. Wilmer retailed these details to Director Carrington-Carr, who said in a rather dazed way "Check." He closed the ledger, handed it to Keeper Gallagher, and turning to the scientists announced: "Gentlemen, believe it or not, every answer agrees with our records, absolutely. Shall we proceed?"

Before proceeding, however, the photographers had to have their inning. They took pictures of Mr. Wilmer shaking hands with Lucy, of Mr. Wilmer with Lucy's trunk around his neck, feeding Lucy a peanut, shaking hands with the Director, shaking hands with Keeper Gallagher, and of all the scientists shaking hands with each other.

Then they proceeded to the Crocodile House and Mr. Wilmer interviewed a crocodile with perfect results: every answer checked exactly with the records in the ledger. During the rest of the afternoon he questioned a camel, a hippopotamus, a wart hog, a boa constrictor, an eagle and an armadillo. As each ques-

tion was answered correctly Mr. Carrington-Carr checked it off in the ledger, his astonishment growing steadily as in a dazed voice he automatically repeated, "Check . . . Check . . . Check." The amazement of the scientists also increased until they even ceased to argue with one another. Several times Keeper Gallagher was seen to cross himself.

The only upset came when Mr. Wilmer attempted to question a Siberian Bear. He was a great towering fellow and seemed friendly enough and eager to talk, but William Wilmer couldn't understand a word of what he said, although he repeated it several times. Puzzled, he turned to Mr. Carrington-Carr. "I just can't understand him," he said. "He keeps saying something that sounds like '*Ne govoru po Angliski.*'"

"What was that?" one of the scientists asked quickly. William Wilmer repeated it as well as he could.

"Why that is Russian," the scientist explained excitedly. "That is Russian for 'No speak English.'"

"Glory be!" shouted Keeper Gallagher. "Of course it would be. He's only been here a week, come Monday. Just off the boat he is and how could the poor beast be learning to talk American in them few days?"

Director Carrington-Carr slammed the ledger shut and started toward the office. "Come, gentlemen," he said; "I think you will agree that this phenomenon has been proven beyond the shadow of a doubt."

When they were all back in the Director's office and the newsmen had been locked out, Mr. Carrington-Carr began: "Gentlemen, what we have just witnessed seems utterly fantastic, impossible, unbelievable — and yet — it seems to be true. I just do not know *what* to think — "

"*I* think," said William Wilmer weakly, "I'd like to go home."

The Director suddenly noticed that he was quite pale and seemed about to faint again. "Oh, I'm so sorry," he said hastily. "We really have put you through quite an exhausting day." He went to a cupboard and brought Mr. Wilmer a small glass of brandy. "Here, take this, it will do you good."

William Wilmer had never tasted brandy and he choked and sputtered considerably, but it did make him feel better.

"I'll drive the lad home," volunteered Keeper Gallagher. "I've got the jalopy here and I live only a few blocks above his address." He eyed the glass meaningly. "I've not had too easy a day meself, what with Toby and all."

William Wilmer vaguely remembered shaking hands with the Director and all the scientific gentlemen and being led kindly out to Mr. Gallagher's car. He climbed in and promptly went to sleep.

Later, he remembered being waked up at Mrs. Keeler's house; he remembered more flashlights and Mr. Gallagher's officious voice saying, "Make room there and leave the gentleman get to his bed. It's completely exhausted he is, what with conversing all day with the animals and confounding the scientific world and all."

He remembered hearing, as he wearily climbed the stairs to his room, Mr. Gallagher addressing Mr. and Mrs. Keeler. "Shure ma'am, the miracles I've seen and heard this day have me completely unstrung. A glass of beer maybe, to settle me nerves, and I'll tell you events will have your eyes popping out like hard-boiled eggs."

CHAPTER III

Blue Monday

～～～～～～～～～ ～～～～～～～～～

O N MONDAY morning William Wilmer, much refreshed by his long night's sleep, came down to breakfast to find the dining room a sea of newspapers. Mr. Keeler hailed him gaily — "Well, Willie, my boy, you're a celebrity, take a look."

He held up a copy of the *Daily Bleat* and Mr. Wilmer was astonished to see the entire front page devoted to a picture of himself, with his hand in Toby's mouth. Under it, large type said: MODERN DANIEL IN THE LION'S DEN. *Stories on pages 2, 6, 9 and 11. More pictures on pages 3, 5, 15, 18, and 20.*

The *Times* had a picture of him with the Siberian bear and a caption THE MAN WHO TALKS LIKE A BEAR. The *Tribune* displayed him with Lucy's trunk around his neck and a headline INSURANCE CLERK CONFOUNDS SCIENTIFIC WORLD. There were interviews with Director Carrington-Carr, with all the scientists who were present — and a very dramatic one with Keeper Gallagher. There were editorials and expressions of opinion from the Mayor, the Governor, prominent Churchmen (including an Archbishop), the Petroleum Co-ordinator and Shirley Temple.

Many of them declared that it was all nonsense and a great hoax; there were some threats that it would be investigated by a Congressional Committee. But the Director and the scientists, all of whom were most highly respected, united in declaring every word of it to be true.

"It looks like the beginnings of a swell knock-down-and-drag-out con*tro*versy," chuckled Mr. Keeler, rummaging for more pictures. "Better than a murder trial. My lad, you'll be on the front page for a month."

Mrs. Keeler, entering with the coffee, said, "It's a wonder they wouldn't have let you comb your hair before they took all those pictures. You look terrible, and that collar's a sight."

"Here's one that isn't so bad," Mr. Keeler grinned. "This one of him giving a candy bar to the crocodile. At least it's pretty good of the crocodile."

"Pass Mr. Wilmer the sugar and don't be trying to make wisecracks," Mrs. Keeler said. "You're no pin-up boy yourself and he's late now."

Mr. Wilmer glanced at his watch and hastily gulped half of his coffee. "Goodness," he exclaimed, "I certainly am." He hastened out, discovered that his hat was still somewhere at the Zoo and was forced to borrow Mr. Keeler's, which was a size and a half too large. As the front door slammed Mrs. Keeler smiled affectionately. "Isn't he the great one?" she sighed. "Here he is, the most talked-about person in the country — and worrying about being two minutes late to work."

William Wilmer rushed into the lobby of the S. S. & C. Building on the stroke of nine. He would be almost three minutes late, the first time such a thing had happened since the big blizzard six years before. He was so flustered and out of breath that he scarcely noticed the popping of more photographers' flashlights or the jovial greeting of Claude, the starter. Nor, as he hurried down Aisle J to his desk, did he note the smiles and interest of his fellow workers.

He whipped the cover from his calculating machine, put it in the lower right-hand drawer, eased his sleeves and looked up — to see the office boy grinning at him.

"Hi, Daniel," hailed the boy cheerily. "You're wanted in the lion's den." He jerked his thumb over his shoulder. "Twitch; and boy, is he steamed up! Better try some monkey talk on him, he might understand that."

When he entered Mr. Twitch's office William Wilmer found the same confusion of scattered newspapers that had marked the Keeler dining room. Mr. Twitch was stamping up and down and Mr. Partington, Executive Vice President, was stamping up and down and Miss Sweeney was sitting down, with her notebook and pencil. Mr. Twitch was white with rage, Mr. Partington was red with annoyance, and Miss Sweeney was very pink with something, Mr. Wilmer didn't know what.

"*Well*, Wilmer," Mr. Twitch greeted him, "this *is* a fine mess! The Safe, Sane and Colossal Insurance Company, Incorporated, the oldest, most respected firm in the Metropolitan area, employing crazy people, employing madmen! What will people think? What will our competitors say?" He snatched up a newspaper and threw it on the floor. "INSURANCE CLERK CONFOUNDS SCIENTIFIC WORLD. DANIEL IN THE

LION'S DEN. MAN WHO TALKS LIKE A BEAR . . . Bah!" He was so irritated that he blew his nose on his show handkerchief and then threw *that* on the floor. "Next time you see fit to give out any idiotic interviews, Wilmer, you can say that you *were* employed by the Safe, Sane and Colossal Company, do you understand? You *were* employed!"

Mr. Partington, redder than ever, grunted: "Sorry Wilmer, won't do, won't do — *Harumph!* Very bad publicity for the Firm, very bad, have to go, have to go — *Harumph!*" — and stamped out.

"I'm sorry — " William Wilmer began, but Mr. Twitch interrupted him.

"*Sorry!*" he raged. "You're fired, that's what you are. Fired, let go, discharged, dismissed! *Get out!*" And as Mr. Wilmer left he snapped at Miss Sweeney: "Take a memo. Statement to the press — "

But Miss Sweeney had risen and neatly placed her notebook and pencil on the chair. "I'll be back," she said, disdainfully kicking Mr. Twitch's purple-bordered handkerchief out of her path, "when I feel like it" — and followed William Wilmer from the office.

She came up just as he had reached his desk and held out her hand. "Good-by, Mr. Wilmer," she said. "I'm glad you're going."

"*Glad?*" he said, shaking hands confusedly. "Why, *I'm* not; I've been fired, I haven't any job."

Miss Sweeney's nose wrinkled delightfully as she smiled at him. "You certainly are dumb," she chuckled — "but nice. Don't you realize that you've just lost the worst job in the world, that you're *free* — and out of this jail? I wish I were. Don't you realize that you're the most famous person in the United States at this moment?"

"Well — but — " He realized that he was still holding her hand and dropped it hastily. "I still haven't any job. Thanks ever so much though, Miss Sweeney — thanks a lot."

He went through the desk and cleaned out his personal possessions. There weren't many, considering that he had worked there eleven years. There was a broken fountain pen and a pair of spectacles that he used once in a while, a necktie and a pair of gloves that he had bought last week and forgotten to take home. There was an American Legion poppy, an automatic pencil that didn't work, a penknife, a vest-button and two half-rolls of Peppermint Patooties. He wrapped these all neatly in a sheet of typewriter paper, snapped an elastic band around the small package, put the cover on his calculating machine — and left the Safe, Sane and Colossal Insurance Company, Incorporated, for all time.

It seemed strange to be out in the streets on a week-day morning. It was the first time William Wilmer could remember such a thing. In a sort of daze he walked across town and up Fifth Avenue. There were shoppers everywhere, hurrying in and out of stores and looking at the show windows. They all looked so well dressed and prosperous, he wondered where all the money came from.

The thought of money suddenly reminded him that he had forgotten to give Mrs. Keeler his board on Saturday. Oh well, he would pay it tonight and then there would be a few dollars left to last till — *when?* The thought terrified him. There would be no pay envelope this Saturday. There would *never* be an-

other pay envelope until he had found a new job. He
realized that he ought to buy a newspaper at once and
start looking at the Help Wanted columns, for jobs
were scarce these days, as Mr. Twitch had so callously
reminded him, but somehow he just couldn't start on
it right now.

He wandered up the Avenue, looking in the shop
windows without knowing what he saw. He sat for
a while on a bench in the little park behind the Li-
brary. There were a great many bedraggled tramps
sitting there and William Wilmer realized that they
were out of jobs too. "Goodness," he thought, "I
hope I don't look like *that*," and hastily resumed his
wandering.

It was almost noon now, so he had a small lunch in a drugstore and continued to walk. Eventually he reached the Park and was grateful for the shade and the coolness of the water, for the spring weather was continuing warm and he was hot, tired and dusty. He sat a while by the lake and then wandered up to the Lion House; he thought he might as well see how Toby was doing.

The moment he entered the building Keeper Gallagher hailed him — "Good morning, sir, good morning" — and he touched his cap in a half salute. "The Director's been trying to locate you all day. Come right in, he'll be glad to see you." He flung open the door of the Director's office and announced, "Mr. Wilmer to see you, sir."

Mr. Carrington-Carr rose up and shook hands cordially. "Hello, Wilmer," he said. "Glad you showed up. I phoned your house and they said you'd gone to the office, and I phoned the office and they said you'd gone — for good."

"Yes," said William Wilmer, sadly, "I was fired."

"Splendid," laughed the Director, "saves you the trouble of resigning."

Mr. Wilmer didn't see anything splendid about it, so he sat down and waited for Mr. Carrington-Carr to continue, which he did: —

"Wilmer, as you doubtless know, all zoos have many animals who are unhappy, discontented, surly, or really ill. In some cases they, perhaps, do not like their quarters or their neighbors or their diet. In some cases they are homesick or lonesome, in some cases they have a real physical trouble, as Toby did. Not knowing the cause of their unhappiness we are helpless to remedy it. *But*, if you, with this amazing gift of yours, were available to talk with the animals and discuss their troubles, I am sure that we could have here the healthiest and happiest zoo in this country, or in any country.

"With this thought in mind we held a special meeting of the Trustees last night at which I was authorized to offer you the position of Special Animal Consultant to the Central Zoo."

"Why, that sounds very nice," said Mr. Wilmer, not quite comprehending what it was all about. "When shall I go to work and what are the hours?"

"Hours?" he laughed. "There wouldn't be any hours. You would only have to be here when you felt like it, or when some animal required special attention. There is an office here next to mine that you can have, it's quiet and pleasant and you could come and go just as you pleased."

He opened a door and ushered William Wilmer into the adjoining office. It was the pleasantest room he had ever seen, much like the Director's office, but slightly smaller. Broad windows opened on masses of flowering shrubs and a vista of lawns and trees running down to the Lake. There were several comfortable chairs, a couch and a desk. There were bookshelves filled with interesting animal books and even a cozy fireplace piled with birch logs.

"Why — why it's wonderful," Mr. Wilmer stammered, stroking the broad, flat-topped desk. "It doesn't look like an office at all." He opened a drawer and deposited his small package of possessions in it. As he did so his attention was caught by a check placed on the desk blotter. His eyes popped at seeing his own name typed on it and the figures 500 dollars and oo cents.

Mr. Carrington-Carr, who was looking out of the window, spoke over his shoulder. "By the way, the salary is six thousand a year. That's your first month's check, if everything is agreeable to you."

"Agreeable!" gasped Mr. Wilmer and sat down very suddenly in the desk chair. "But — Mr. Carrington-Carr, that's three or four times as much as I was making — I — I really don't need that much." Relief and happiness had made his voice quite shaky and the view from the window somehow seemed to be misty and wavering.

Director Carrington-Carr laughed heartily as he held out his hand. "I'm afraid that you'll have to discover some way of using it, Wilmer; it's the very *least* the Trustees are willing to pay. Well, what do you say? Do you accept our offer?"

"Accept it?" Mr. Wilmer cried, his voice still not quite under control. "Goodness gracious yes. I should say so!"

Mr. Wilmer went home to Mrs. Keeler's in such a state of elation that he seemed to be floating through the air. "My," he smiled to himself, "I hope I'm not developing *another* remarkable talent. One's plenty."

As he approached the house he was aware that there was quite a crowd around the front steps. He recognized the now familiar cameras and flashlights of reporters, but there were many others too, a perfect swarm of boys and girls. He was recognized and they fairly mobbed him, holding out dirty little autograph albums and slips of paper and all shouting, "Give us yer autograph Mister; c'm on, give us yer autograph." Mr. Wilmer managed to struggle

through them and mount the steps, where he found Mr. Keeler holding forth to the newsmen. "Hi, Willie," he called jovially. "Come and join the party. I've just been giving the boys a few home-life details about you; you know — what you eat for breakfast, when you go to bed — that sort of stuff."

They all asked questions at once and William Wilmer answered as well as he could. He told them where he had gone to school and when and what he had studied. He told them that he had once had pet white mice and that he wore size eight-and-a-half shoes. He told them the names of his favorite breakfast food, shaving soap, toothpaste and movie actress. That the *Daily Bleat* was his favorite newspaper and Peppermint Patooties his favorite candy. That he liked sweet potatoes, but didn't care for Brussels sprouts.

It looked as though he would be kept there the rest of the afternoon, until he suddenly had a bright idea. "If you gentlemen want a new story," he said, "you ought to go over and see Director Carrington-Carr. I have just been appointed to an official position at the Zoo, but you will have to get the details from him."

The reporters all dropped their questioning, snatched up their cameras and rushed off looking for taxis. At last Mr. Wilmer could remove Mr. Keeler's hat, mop his perspiring brow and sit down. "I don't suppose anyone has found *my* hat yet?" he inquired.

"Yes," Mr. Keeler answered. "One of them reporters brought it. Found it in the alligator's cage. It don't look like much." He opened the door and added, "Come on in Willie, lots more inside."

Mr. Wilmer found the living room packed with people. Mrs. Keeler, seated in her rocker, was having a lovely time telling all the gentlemen about her childhood in Lynn, Massachusetts, and about Mr. Wilmer and what a nice lodger he was. Her lap was filled with telegrams and air-mail letters. "Come right in, Mr. Wilmer," she called as he hesitated in the hall, "a few gentlemen to see you."

The gentlemen immediately swarmed upon him, presenting cards, waving contracts and all talking at once. They were almost as bad as the autograph seekers. It was all so confusing that it took Mr. Wilmer some time to discover who they were and what they wanted, but eventually he got them somewhat straightened out. Three were lecture agents and four were movie scouts looking for new talent. There were six from advertising agencies, seeking his endorsement of various products. There were five radio scouts from the leading broadcasting companies, two literary agents, representatives of three publishing houses and one man who had just wandered in to see what was going on. Then there were four women and five men, each of whom wanted to become Wilmer's personal manager.

One of the latter backed Mr. Wilmer into a corner and shoved everyone else away. "Listen Bud," he said threateningly, "don't pay no attention to them lugs, *I'm* your man. Why, I've managed Kid McSlug and Daffy Tony and Slap-em-dead Levine." He extended a rather grimy card. "Eddie Offenbacker, that's me, and I can put you into the big money."

"But — I'm not a prize fighter," protested Mr. Wilmer.

"Don't matter," answered the man. "I can manage *anything*."

"Well, suppose you manage to clear out of here and leave Mr. Wilmer be," suggested Mr. Keeler, picking up a heavy umbrella stand.

"Oh, yeah?" the man began, but seeing Mrs. Keeler quietly toying with a pair of fire tongs, reluctantly left.

William Wilmer thought of Mr. Carrington-Carr and how easily he handled such situations. Determined to be as much like the Director as possible, he rapped on the table for attention. "Gentlemen," he announced firmly, "I must inform you that I am at present employed as Special Animal Consultant of the Central Zoo. I do not need any managers, agents, contracts or jobs. If you will kindly leave your cards and offers on the hall table as you go out, I shall consider them when I have the opportunity. You may communicate with me at my office any Monday afternoon between two and four."

They all started talking and shoving again, but noting that Mr. Keeler continued to hold his umbrella stand and that Mrs. Keeler still toyed with the fire tongs, they gradually filed out. There was quite a stack of papers left on the hall table, and these Mr. Wilmer put in a cardboard shoe box which he tied with a bit of string. Now that things were quiet he sat down with a tired sigh, but at once Mrs. Keeler dumped her collection of telegrams and air-mail letters in his lap, saying, "You might as well get started on these, they've been coming all day and there'll be another batch along soon. And the telephone's been ringing steady, till I stuck a wad of paper in it."

It took all three of them some time to get the envelopes separated into some sort of order, then Mr. Wilmer started to read them. There were telegrams from the zoos of Chicago, Detroit, San Francisco, Washington and Atlanta, from two circuses, and from a private menagerie in Hollywood. All of these asked Mr. Wilmer to act as Special Consultant and offered salaries of from five to ten thousand dollars per year.

There were more offers from radio stations, advertising agencies, magazines and lecture bureaus. There were three telegrams from phonograph companies who wanted him to make records in Animal. There was one from *Who's Which in the U. S.* asking for a biographical sketch, a photograph and ten dollars. Then there were a great many ads and circulars from clipping bureaus, jewelry, real estate and bond salesmen, and a great number from sanitariums for the feebleminded.

"Oh dear, I can never answer all of these," Mr. Wilmer exclaimed helplessly.

"Haven't you a filing cabinet in that new office of yours?" Mrs. Keeler suggested. "That's the best way to get rid of them. Keeler, get Mr. Wilmer another shoe box — better get two, there'll be another batch shortly — and take that paper out of the telephone bell."

Mr. Keeler fetched the shoe boxes and released the telephone bell, which immediately began to ring violently. He answered it, then placed his hand over the mouthpiece and turned to the others. "It's her again," he said wearily.

"Who's her?" began Mr. Wilmer.

"Mrs. Protheroe Plushington, that's who," Mrs. Keeler explained. "You know; her picture's always in the paper. High society stuff, richest dame in New York, carries her jewels in a trailer — and a nut, if you ask me. Well, *she's* been on the phone, her doctor's been on the phone, her attorney's been on the phone, her secretary's been on the phone, her veterinary's been on the phone — and her Rolls Royce has been waiting outside the house here half the day — for *you*."

"Pale blue," Mr. Keeler joined in, "and long as a freight car. Chauffeur and footman in blue livery, looked like doormen down to the Roxy. Every kid in the neighborhood around here looking at it. It's there again," he added, glancing out of the front window.

"Isn't the lady waiting?" asked Mr. Wilmer, nervously eying the telephone.

"Leave her wait," said Mr. Keeler, and his wife took up the recital.

"It seems she's got a sick pooch, a Pekinee, name of Frou-Frou — that name ought to make it sick, let alone anything else. Anyway, nobody knows what's ailing the little darling. The lady's coming down with hysterics, the vet's about to be fired, the secretary's got the jitters and they all want William Wilmer. She lives at the Giltdorf Towers — she would."

"Dear me," said William Wilmer, "I guess I'd better go over and see if I can do anything."

Mr. Keeler uncovered the mouthpiece, said, "O.K. he's coming," hung up the receiver and suggested, "Say, I'd certainly enjoy a ride in that buggy. How's about if I went along to —"

"How's about," Mrs. Keeler said icily, "if you give Mr. Wilmer his hat — your hat — and take those boxes up to his room and put some coal on the water heater? Then come back and I'll tell you how's about what else."

"Yes my dear," said Mr. Keeler.

The footman helped Mr. Wilmer into the great car and they glided swiftly down to the Giltdorf Towers. There the footman sprang out, guided him through the lobby and into an elevator which whisked them to the forty-seventh floor. Cap in hand he led the way to the door of Mrs. Plushington's apartment where Mr. Wilmer was eagerly met by an agitated butler, a maid who had obviously been crying and a secretary who had been, and still was, perspiring. They escorted him to the living room, which was the largest room he had ever seen — except the Grand Central waiting room or the main office of the Safe, Sane and Colossal Company. There they were joined by Mrs. Plushington's attorney, Mrs. Plushington's doctor and

Mrs. Plushington's veterinary. All of them began to talk at once and William Wilmer couldn't make head or tail of what they were saying. He was very tired by now, it was long past his dinnertime; he was hungry and, for him, quite cross.

"Gentlemen," he said, remembering Mr. Carrington-Carr, "if I could just see the dog and talk with her — "

The veterinary interrupted sulkily, "If *I* could talk to her — "

"Well, you can't," snapped the attorney, "and Mr. Wilmer can — we hope; so let's go" — and he led them all into Mrs. Plushington's bedroom.

It was slightly smaller than the living room, but much fancier. Everything seemed to be blue and pink, including Mrs. Plushington, who was lying on a large, frilly bed. Her negligee was blue and her eyes and nose were very pink. A nurse stood beside her bed, with a bottle of smelling salts in one hand and a fan in the other.

The Pekinese lay in a sort of elaborate cradle affair, also done in pink and blue with lots of lace and ribbons. It reminded Mr. Wilmer of a newsreel he had seen showing the Crown Prince of Bulgravia in his state cradle. The dog, if it could be called that, lay on its side panting painfully. Its runny eyes were closed, its very fur seemed limp, but it did manage a faint snarl as William Wilmer knelt down and said

in his small Animal voice, "Well, Frou-Frou, you don't seem to be very well, what's wrong?"

She roused slightly and her voice came, sharp and irritable, as she turned her pop-eyes on him. "Well, it's about time they found someone who could talk. Where have *you* been all my life? Why don't you tell that glass-eyed imbecile what's ailing me? Why don't you *tell* him I ate a mule?"

"*Ate a mule?*" Mr. Wilmer cried, gazing in astonishment at the tiny beast. "Goodness gracious, where would *you* find a mule and how — "

" 'Slipper' to you, idiot — that's what they call them here. One of hers. Red morocco leather, lined with swan's-down — ugh! And that beetle-brained vet has been giving me loathsome vitamins and injections and sunrays when all I need is a stomach pump — *and* quickly."

William Wilmer rose and announced, "She's eaten a red morocco slipper and she wants a stomach pump," and then he sat down in a comfortable chair, for he was very tired.

Mrs. Protheroe Plushington rose in her bed and screamed, "*So*, Clemencine, that's where that slipper went! Why didn't you tell me, you wicked, deceitful creature?" She picked up a bedside lamp and hurled it at the maid, but Clemencine dodged and the lamp shattered a huge mirror.

The veterinary and his assistant hastily carried Frou-Frou's cradle out to a bathroom, Mrs. Plushington collapsed again, her doctor and nurse hurried to her bedside, her secretary continued to perspire and William Wilmer continued to sit in the comfortable chair. He was getting sleepy now.

After a short time the veterinary tiptoed in and approached Mrs. Plushington's bed. "It *was* a slipper," he admitted. "Red morocco. . . . She's all right now."

They brought the crib back with Frou-Frou lying as limply as before, but breathing more easily. Mrs. Plushington went into hysterics again and William Wilmer knelt down and spoke to Frou-Frou. "Feeling all right now?" he asked.

"Of course I'm not feeling all right, imbecile," she snarled weakly, without opening her eyes. "But I *am* a lot better. If these hysterical morons will just let me get a good night's sleep I'll be all right in the morning. And as soon as I get my strength back I'm going to tear a finger off that half-witted vet if it's the last act of my life. Go 'way."

He informed Mrs. Plushington that Frou-Frou merely needed a good sleep and advised them not to let her be disturbed before morning. He started to go, but Mrs. Plushington clasped his hand in both of hers and turned her tear-streaked face up to him. It was not a pretty face at best, and her hands were hot and fat and damp. William Wilmer felt very foolish.

"Dear *dear* Mr. Wilmer," she cried. "How can I *ever* thank you enough? You saved my precious darling's life, and mine too, for I could *never* exist without her." The thought set her weeping again, but she turned to her secretary and snapped, "My checkbook." He handed her a gold fountain pen and a checkbook bound in blue satin. She dropped Mr. Wilmer's hand long enough to write a check, tore it out and handed it to him. His jaw dropped and his eyes bulged slightly as he saw the figures — 5000 dollars and 00 cents!

He murmured weakly, "Thank you very much, Mrs. Plushington, thank you very much indeed!" — and put the check in his pocket. "Well, I guess I'd

better be going — " he began, but she got hold of his hand again and went on: "Dear *dear* Mr. Wilmer, I know it is asking a *great* deal, but could you, *would* you consider coming to Frou-Frou and me for perhaps an hour once a week, let us say Sunday evenings at nine, and having a little three-cornered chat with us? You see — my darling and I have never *quite* attained that *perfect*, sympathetic understanding which I so *deeply* desire. If, with your *miraculous* gift, you could convey to me her dear *dear* thoughts and desires, and mine to her, I am *sure* our soul union would be made *complete*."

"Why of course," answered William Wilmer. "I would be very glad to."

"You dear, *dear* generous lad," she cooed delightedly. "You have been *so* kind to us. And oh — stupid me — I have forgotten to mention any retainer. Would you, could you, *dear* Mr. Wilmer, consider a thousand dollars a month sufficient? I know it is a miserable, niggardly pittance for one with your *miraculous* talents, but what with the taxes and everything poor Frou-Frou and I are practically *destitute*."

"Why of course — why — yes indeed," Mr. Wilmer agreed, dizzily. "Well, I guess I'd better be going."

"*Au revoir*, then," she called, "until Sunday — you wonderful, *wonderful* person."

Frou-Frou snored peacefully; the butler handed Mr. Wilmer Mr. Keeler's hat and the secretary escorted him down to the car. The secretary had ceased to perspire now and while the footman held open the door he shook Mr. Wilmer's hand cordially. "Thanks ever so much, old man," he said, "for all you've done. If anything had happened to that filthy little beast old Plush would have had someone's scalp and I've a feeling it might have been mine. You see, *I* gave Frou-Frou that confounded slipper to play with."

As William Wilmer climbed wearily to his room, he felt that it had been the longest day of his life — and the most eventful. It seemed incredible that so much had occurred in only three days. Only three days ago he had been working for the Safe, Sane and Colossal Company! Only three days ago he had first heard an Animal voice — the Policeman's horse. Only this morning he had been discharged and had wandered the streets, out of work, discouraged and wondering when he would ever see another pay envelope. And now he had the pleasantest position that anyone could imagine, a salary that he could hardly comprehend and so much money that it made him dizzy when he thought of it. He was completely exhausted but wonderfully happy. "My," he thought. "Things certainly do happen quickly."

There were two more shoe boxes of telegrams and letters in his room, but he didn't bother to look at them. He opened his top bureau drawer and put the Director's check and Mrs. Plushington's check in the cigar box where he kept his High School diploma, his class pin, and a typewriter eraser that Miss Sweeney had once dropped on the floor. He had picked it up when she wasn't looking and had kept it ever since.

CHAPTER IV

William Whistles

W HEN HIS ALARM
went off at 6:45 the next morning, William Wilmer
leaped up and shut it off as usual, stumbled to the
bathroom as usual, and was half shaved before he *remembered*.

He didn't *have* to be at the S. S. & C. office at 8:57!
He didn't *have* to be *anywhere* at 8:57, or any other
time! He almost decided to go back to bed and loll a
while, just to see how it felt, but the spring sunshine
was too inviting; he was far too excited to lie abed.
It was the first time in years that he had waked up
in the morning and really looked forward to a day
with pleasant thrills. Besides, he suddenly recollected,
he hadn't had any dinner last night and was ravenously
hungry.

As he burst into the dining room Mr. Keeler
greeted him with, "Good morning, Mr. Special Con-

sultant," and waved at the scattered newspapers. Again, all the front pages were mostly devoted to William Wilmer. There were accounts of his appointment to the Zoo staff, and pictures of him and Director Carrington-Carr and of their offices. There were new controversies between prominent people over his great gift, and opinions from the Secretary of the Navy, the Bishop of Canterbury and the Nobel Prize Committee.

There was also a long interview with Mrs. Protheroe Plushington, accompanied by pictures of Frou-Frou, Frou-Frou in her cradle and Mrs. Plushington in diamonds. Mr. Wilmer could hardly recognize her as the tear-stained object he had seen last night, but Mrs. Keeler, looking over his shoulder, explained with a sniff: "That was taken a good twenty years ago; look at the dress she's wearing. Why those went out before the Depression."

William Wilmer was much more interested in his breakfast than he was in the papers and he was more interested in getting away from Mrs. Keeler's house than in either, for already a messenger boy had left a new handful of telegrams, any moment the telephone would begin to ring, and there would be more reporters. He gathered up the four shoe boxes and hastened forth, hatless. Mr. Keeler's hat was really pretty ridiculous, and the alligators had quite ruined his own.

As the front door slammed, Mrs. Keeler turned

awestruck eyes on her husband. "Did you hear that?" she asked in a hushed voice.

"I did," he answered. "Whistling!"

"Yes, whistling," she mused thoughtfully — "the first time I've heard him whistle in going on eleven years."

The trip to the Zoo was only a fairly short bus ride, so it was still quite early when William Wilmer arrived there. Keeper Gallagher, who was sprinkling the gravel paths outside the offices, greeted him cheerily. "My, my, Mr. Wilmer," he said, "you're early indeed. The Director himself seldom comes before nine or ten. But it's a lovely morning and the early part's always the best part."

"I guess it is," agreed Mr. Wilmer. "How's Toby?"

"Fine as can be. Frisky as a kitten and good as a lamb. Drop by and have a chat with him, he'll enjoy seeing you." He paused as a distant trumpeting sounded. "And there's Lucy knows you've come and she'll be wanting a word too. You'll be a busy man here, Mr. Wilmer, what with all the animals and them wanting a good talk now and then, and a happy one, too, I think."

"I'm sure I will," Mr. Wilmer said. "I certainly am now."

His office was even pleasanter than he remembered. The windows were open; outside, the shrubs, now bursting into bloom, were being eagerly investigated by hungry bees. A pair of robins, with a great deal of argument, were building a nest in a maple tree; from the cages and runs and houses came a contented chorus of moos, grunts, roars, cluckings, and chatterings, as the animals talked over their breakfasts and reveled in the spring sunshine.

William Wilmer untied the shoe boxes and went to work on his correspondence. He placed all the telegrams from zoos and circuses in one pile; in another pile he put all the vaudeville, radio and movie offers. Another pile contained all the advertisers' requests for his endorsements, another the offers from lecture agents, while the largest collection consisted of the advertisements for sanitariums, begging letters, requests for autographs and letters from cranks. This latter pile he just dumped into the scrapbasket; then he plunged into reading the others. He had hardly begun when the Director strolled in and greeted him cheerily. "Good Heavens," he said, glancing at the cluttered desk, "what's all this?"

"I guess you'd call it fan mail," Mr. Wilmer smiled, a bit sheepishly. He explained what the piles consisted of and how they were separated. "I wish," he added helplessly, "that sometime when you are not too busy you would give me some advice about these, I don't know what to do about them."

"No time like the present," laughed Mr. Carrington-Carr. "I'd be delighted to, it isn't often I have an opportunity to pry into a celebrity's fan mail." He glanced quickly through the zoo pile and continued, "I should accept all the zoo and circus offers. It would be a great kindness to the animals and a huge help to the directors. They're all fine chaps, I know most of them, and you'll enjoy meeting them. But accept on a basis of two visits a year, then every six months we'll work out a schedule and you can make a swing around the country and clean up the whole thing in three weeks or so. They'll be pleasant trips, do you enjoy travel?"

"Yes indeed," answered Mr. Wilmer eagerly. "Well — that is — I never have really *gone* anywhere, but I've always wanted to."

"You will," said Mr. Carrington-Carr, smiling kindly. "You are going places, lots of them. Well, what's next?"

Next was the lecture pile and the Director, after glancing at a few of them, laid them back on the desk. "I would advise," he said firmly, "no lectures. They'd take entirely too much of your time and the agent would get most of the money — "

"And I couldn't possibly lecture anyway," finished Mr. Wilmer, and dropped *those* in the scrapbasket. "Then there are these requests for testimonials," he went on. "They offer lots of money, but I've never used any of these things or had any of them and I

don't see how I could sign them honestly."

"Let's see," said the Director. "Here's Dromedary Cigarettes — *After a hard day of interviewing animals nothing is as relaxing as a Dromedary. They are 85 per cent tobacco. I never smoke any other brand. Signed,* WILLIAM WILMER. Well, what's wrong with that?"

"But I don't smoke *anything*," protested William Wilmer.

Mr. Carrington-Carr laughed and offered his cigarette case saying, "Here, light up." William Wilmer did so, very awkwardly, took one puff and immediately sneezed, coughed, strangled and choked, while the Director roared with laughter. William Wilmer wiped his eyes and the Director, wiping his, said, "There now, that was a Dromedary. You've never smoked any other brand, have you? Sign on the dotted line. After all, thirty-five hundred dollars isn't to be sneezed at, even if Dromedaries are."

Next was Eichelslaub's Beer — *Eichelslaub's is my favorite beer. Signed*, WILLIAM WILMER.

"But I've never tasted beer," he protested.

"Well, you will," smiled Mr. Carrington-Carr. "We'll have a glass of Eichelslaub's for lunch; then it will be your favorite, naturally. Oh, wait a minute, they're only offering two thousand dollars; let's see if we can't do better. My, this is fun," he chuckled, as he glanced through the papers. "Here's a better one, Speiler's Beer — three thousand dollars. Fine, *Speiler's* Beer will be your favorite. Sign Speiler's."

In this manner they went through all the testimonials. There were mattresses, radios, refrigerators, toothpastes, razors, hotels and a dozen other things which William Wilmer signed as his favorites.

"Well, that settles the testimonials," the Director said. He jotted down the amounts, added them up and whistled. "Thirty-six thousand, five hundred!" he exclaimed. "That's certainly a good morning's work, Wilmer. What else is there?"

He glanced through the radio and movie offers and advised, "Better let these rest awhile; you shouldn't get *too* involved right now. Any more?" When Mr. Wilmer explained that he had thrown the rest in the scrapbasket, he nodded approvingly. "That's the place for them; you're learning rapidly. Now I should say that the first thing is to write your letters of acceptance to the zoos. I've had some paper printed for you, by the way, upper left-hand drawer."

William Wilmer opened the drawer and beheld neat stacks of writing paper and envelopes, all engraved CENTRAL ZOO, *Administrative Offices;* and in smaller letters WILLIAM WILMER, SPECIAL CONSULTANT.

"It's wonderful, Mr. Carrington-Carr," he exclaimed. "I've never had any paper of my own before, but I hate to take all this time on my own affairs, I ought to be working for the Zoo."

"Nonsense," laughed the Director. "You've only been here about three hours, and there's nothing urgent. You might stop and have a chat with the black panther when you get time, Gallagher tells me she's been sulky lately, that's all."

Left alone, Mr. Wilmer took out a sheet of his new paper and prepared to write to the San Francisco Zoo. Then he suddenly thought of Miss Sweeney. He

thought of her encouraging smile and her firm hand-
clasp when she said good-by. (Could it have been
only yesterday morning?) He thought of how the
light had glinted in her red hair and of how deep the
blue of her eyes was, and of the entrancing way her
nose had wrinkled. So on the first sheet of his new
stationery he wrote: —

My dear Miss Sweeney: —

I just wanted to let you know that I have a fine position here at the Central Zoo. Mr. Carrington-Carr, the
Director, is the nicest man I have ever known. Mr. Gallagher is nice and the animals are all nice too, especially
the lion, Toby. Hoping that everything is well with you,
I remain,

Yours truly,

WILLIAM WILMER

When it came to addressing the envelope he realized
that he didn't know her first name, so he had to just
write *Miss Sweeney, Dep't HJ6, S. S. & C. Ins. Co.*
Then he began on the San Francisco Zoo letter.

He had hardly started, however, when the Director
popped in again. "Wilmer," he said, "an old friend of
mine, Charlie Pulpwood, just called up. Wants us to
have lunch with him at the Yalevard Club. He's Editor of the *Post Companion*, anxious to meet you."

"Thank you, that would be very nice," answered

Mr. Wilmer, and then, remembering, "But I haven't any hat. The alligators rather spoiled mine."

"That's all right," laughed Mr. Carrington-Carr. "I have to stop at Creeks's anyway, and we'll get you one there, compliments of the Zoo."

On the way downtown in a taxi William Wilmer told Mr. Carrington-Carr of his experience last evening, with Mrs. Plushington, Frou-Frou and the slipper. The Director laughed until his eyes filled with tears. "My, my, Wilmer," he chuckled. "You certainly *are* going places. And a thousand a month as a retainer! Why that's twelve thousand a year, just twice what we can pay you. I hope you're not going to desert us for the Giltdorf Towers."

"Don't worry," smiled William Wilmer. "You've never seen Frou-Frou — *or* Mrs. Protheroe Plushington."

At Creeks's they selected a new hat and Mr. Wilmer was astonished at the difference it made in his appearance. His hats had always been too stiff and the wrong color and always looked somewhat too small, although the clerks had told him that they were perfect. They were "Frat Fello Headgear" priced at $2.98, and the advertisements said that no finer hat could be bought at any price. Mr. Wilmer suddenly realized that advertisements were not always strictly truthful. Greatly pleased with the effect of the hat, he recklessly proposed buying a suit. "You see," he explained, "Mr. Twitch would not stand for our wearing anything but very conservative business clothes at the office."

"You certainly obeyed orders," smiled the Director. "Fine. Let's go suiting." They went upstairs and he introduced Mr. Wilmer to the manager of the suit department.

"Not *the* Mr. Wilmer," asked the manager delightedly, "the — if you will pardon me — The Man Who Talks like a Bear?"

"The very same," said the Director, "and at the moment he's saying 'Woof-Woof, I want a suit, and in a hurry.' "

The manager summoned two salesmen and hurriedly departed. They were shown so many suits that Mr. Wilmer was fairly dizzy trying to make up his mind. He tried to pick one as nearly like Mr. Carrington-Carr's as possible, and the choice finally narrowed down to two. They were both loose-fitting rough tweeds, one bluish gray and the other a tannish gray.

"Why don't you take both?" suggested the Director.

William Wilmer had never owned two new suits at once and the thought was rather startling, but he gamely agreed.

"The bluish one fits perfectly without alterations, would you care to wear it now, Mr. Wilmer?" the clerk inquired. "We can have it pressed a bit and ready for you in ten minutes."

"That would be fine," he said, and then as the clerk

hurried away he suddenly exclaimed: "But goodness gracious, I haven't any money, only last week's pay envelope, it's about twenty-nine dollars!"

Again the Director enjoyed a hearty laugh. "My, you're wonderful Wilmer, perfectly priceless; twenty-nine dollars in pocket and five thousand, five hundred in your bureau drawer. The most famed person in America at the moment and worried about paying for a couple of suits. Well, don't worry, I imagine it can be arranged," he concluded with mock seriousness. "I'm known here; I don't think we'll be arrested."

It was arranged even more easily than he had anticipated, for at that moment the manager reappeared, escorting a very impressive gentleman who was introduced as Mr. Creeks himself.

"This *is* an honor, Mr. Wilmer," he puffed, "a *very* great honor indeed. We deeply appreciate the fact that you have chosen to patronize our establishment. We appreciate it so deeply, in fact, that should you care to continue to favor us exclusively with your patronage and *if* you would not object to our mentioning the fact in our advertisements (all in a very dignified way, of course) Creeks's would be delighted, simply *delighted* to supply all your requirements in the way of clothing, shoes, haberdashery *and* accessories for, let us say, the next year, at no cost to you whatever."

"Fine," exclaimed Director Carrington-Carr, "we accept, but remember, Creeks, you're getting a bargain. Mr. Wilmer's usual price for an endorsement is five thousand per. However, I'll do my best to see that he gets his money's worth. Come along, William," he laughed. "Let's look at some neckties while they press that suit. I could use a few myself."

They picked out several beautiful neckties and, at Mr. Carrington-Carr's suggestion, a few shirts. "Anything else," he asked gaily — "shoes, socks, pajamas, luggage?" — and then, glancing at his watch, "No, we're late now, let's save those for another day."

Mr. Wilmer donned the new suit and one of the new neckties. Looking in the three-sided mirror he was amazed at the unfamiliar person he saw there. It

didn't look at all like the William Wilmer of last
week, which was a great comfort.

"Wonderful," laughed the Director, slapping Mr.
Creeks on the shoulder. "You're wonderful Creeks,
you've produced a completely new man. Come on
William, we're late."

"Better spring this change gently on Toby," he
joked as they went down in the elevator. "He might
not recognize you, and that would be just too bad."

At the Yalevard Club they were met by Mr. Pulpwood, who proved to be a round, red-faced, jolly
person, not at all what Mr. Wilmer had expected an
Editor to be. He had rather dreaded the luncheon,
but both Mr. Pulpwood and the Director were so
friendly and easygoing that he didn't mind it at all.
In fact he enjoyed it very much indeed.

His ability to talk with animals had given him a
little confidence in talking with humans, and when
Mr. Carrington-Carr asked him to retell the story of
his evening with Mrs. Plushington and Frou-Frou he
did so very effectively. So effectively, in fact, that
Mr. Pulpwood laughed and sputtered until he was so
red in the face that the headwaiter hastened over,
thinking that he had choked on a fish bone. Encour-
aged by their interest he also told them about first
hearing the Policeman's horse speak and about the
S. S. & C. Company and Mr. Twitch and Mr. and
Mrs. Keeler, in fact he told them about almost every-

thing he knew — except Miss Sweeney; he didn't mention her.

When they were having dessert Mr. Pulpwood suddenly became more serious. "Mr. Wilmer," he said, "this gift of yours, of being able to converse with animals, is, as you doubtless know, the most remarkable phenomenon of modern times. Our magazine, the *Post Companion* (circulation nine million, six hundred and forty-seven), would like very much to have you write a series of personal interviews with various animals."

"But I couldn't do that," protested Mr. Wilmer. "Goodness, I couldn't write anything, I'm not an author!"

"That is just why we want them," said Mr. Pulpwood earnestly. "We don't *want* anything written by an author; we have too much of that stuff now. What we want is the animals' own simple words, their own stories, their childhood recollections, their trip to this country, their impressions of America, of our buildings, of American women. Why, it would be sensational! We could pay three thousand apiece for, say, a series of twelve, one each month. They would be illustrated by Bullington Livingston, the great animal painter."

William Wilmer had just taken a large spoonful of ice cream and could only gaze out of the window, but the Director cried, "Three thousand! Why Charlie, you piker! Don't you realize that Wilmer gets more than that for merely sleeping on a Beauty Feather Mattress? Why, Dromedary Cigarettes just paid him three thousand, five hundred for taking one puff of a Dromedary! No sir! Not one cent less than six thousand dollars apiece."

"Three thousand," said Mr. Pulpwood. "What do you say, Wilmer?"

"Why — er — " said Mr. Wilmer, having finally swallowed his ice cream. "But I don't spell very well and I never know what to do about commas."

"Damn the commas," shouted Mr. Pulpwood. "Four thousand, that's our limit."

"Six thousand!" shouted Mr. Carrington-Carr.

"Four thousand!" shouted Mr. Pulpwood, still louder. "What's your figure, Wilmer?"

"Well — er — if no one else wants it," he gulped, "five thousand."

"Settled," said Mr. Pulpwood, relaxing and lighting a fresh cigar. "We'll send you a contract and an advance check for the first article tomorrow. Let's have some more coffee."

When they arrived back at the Zoo, Director Carrington-Carr said: "Suppose we have a chat with that black panther, William. I'm a bit worried about her; Gallagher says she's very irritable. Her name's Lola."

Lola *did* look irritable. She was batting at an ant on the floor of her cage. Every time she batted, the

ant wisely scuttled into a crack and Lola's great black
tail lashed the floor with angry thumps.

"Well, Lola," William Wilmer said, in his small
Animal voice, "I hear that you are unhappy about
something. What is it? Aren't you well?"

Lola's pale yellow eyes gleamed venomously from
the black velvet mask of her face as she replied
sharply: "Well? Of course I'm well, why shouldn't
I be well? It's sleep *I* need." She flicked her head
disdainfully toward the next cage. "It's that puma,
the overfed, stupid, sedentary slug! *He snores!* He
snores perfectly horribly most of the day and all of
the night. I haven't had a decent night's sleep in going on six weeks."

"Oh, is that all?" said Mr. Wilmer.

"*All!*" she snarled. "Young man, have you ever
slept next to a snoring puma?"

"Why — er — no, I don't think I ever have," he
admitted.

"Well, try it sometime," she snapped, and went
back to batting the ant.

William Wilmer explained things to the Director, who promptly called Keeper Gallagher. "Gallagher," he said, "move Lola to Cage Twenty-nine over in the corner. She says she can't sleep here."

"Yes, sir," said Keeper Gallagher, and then, smiling approvingly at Mr. Wilmer's new clothes, he observed: "Well Glory be, if it isn't Mr. Wilmer! And me thinking it was maybe Walter Pidgeon or Mr. Anthony Eden himself, perhaps, had come to look at the animals!"

As they walked back toward the offices Director Carrington-Carr said, "Well, William, your first day here has been quite a hectic one. I don't think we'll have to keep you as busy as this ordinarily."

"Busy?" said William Wilmer. "Why, this has been the happiest day of my life!"

Through the late afternoon sunshine there came a shrill but mellow trumpeting. "That's Lucy," he added. "I think I'd better stop and speak to her, she loves to talk. Good night sir, and thanks ever so much — for everything."

CHAPTER V

Strike Up the Band

WHEN HE ARRIVED home Mr. Wilmer found two more shoe boxes of telegrams and letters, and the Keelers, very much dressed-up. Mrs. Keeler wore a large corsage of assorted flowers, while her husband sported a gardenia in his buttonhole. "We didn't think you'd mind," she explained, "there's so many" — and waved at several vases of beautiful flowers that decorated the living room.

"Must have set the old girl back thirty bucks, at least," commented Mr. Keeler. "Came in the blue freight car. Here's the card."

Mr. Wilmer opened a small envelope and read: *To my dear,* DEAR *Mr. Wilmer, with intense gratitude and happy anticipation of our Sunday evening tête-à-tête, from a much improved —* FROU-FROU.

"What's a tayty-tate?" asked Mr. Keeler.

"I can't imagine," answered William Wilmer. "Maybe it's supper."

When, after dinner, Mrs. Keeler proposed that they go to the movies, her husband winked at Mr. Wilmer. "Now ain't that just like a woman?" he smiled. "Just give her flowers and she's got to go places."

"All the flowers you ever gave me," she observed, "wouldn't have got me as far as the end of that rug."

Mr. Wilmer didn't feel especially like a movie, but the telephone was beginning to ring again, and a lady reporter from the *Daily Bleat* was on her way up for an interview, so he decided to go along. He thought it might be restful, but the very first thing shown was a newsreel, and most of it was devoted to William Wilmer. There were pictures of him and Toby, and of Lucy with her trunk around his neck, and of the alligator and of the Siberian bear. The news commentator made lots of remarks that he seemed to think were very humorous, but which made Mrs. Keeler quite indignant. She was also much put out because they hadn't let Mr. Wilmer comb his hair.

"It's an outrage," she declared. "You look terrible."
Mr. Keeler, however, was so swollen with pride that
only with considerable difficulty was he prevented
from announcing their companion's identity to half
the surrounding audience. Mr. Wilmer, burning with
embarrassment, was glad when it was over.

On the way home they stopped at the drugstore
and he treated them to ice-cream sundaes. "My, this
is a party," said Mrs. Keeler, preening herself and
admiring her corsage in the mirror. "Ice cream *and*
flowers! The way to a man's heart may be through
his stomach, as they say, but the way to a woman's
is through flowers."

"Always remember that, Willie," said Mr. Keeler,
solemnly wiping a bit of marshmallow sauce from his
mustache. "Always say it with flowers."

"If you'd say a little more with flowers and a little
less with that big mouth of yours," reminded his wife
tartly, "you'd get farther. And what's more, the name
is Wilmer, to you — *Mr.* Wilmer."

For some days now, workmen had been building
a huge grandstand on the Avenue, directly opposite
the Park entrance. On Wednesday morning as William Wilmer approached the Zoo he noticed that it
was all completed, with flags and bunting waving
gaily in the breeze. In the center was the official box,
covered by a striped canopy and decorated with shields

and the great seal of the city. Early as it was, a few people were already gathering, settling themselves in the reviewing stand and taking up places along the sidewalks.

"What's going on?" he inquired of Keeper Gallagher, as the latter greeted him.

"Why, haven't you seen the papers, Mr. Wilmer?" the Keeper replied. "It's a big parade. Official welcome for the President of Paragunia. All sorts of dignitaries going to be in the reviewing stand; the Mayor, the Governor — maybe the First Lady even. It's scheduled to reach here at noon. Better take it in — I'm going to. There's nothing I like like a good parade."

William Wilmer liked parades too, although it had been a long time since he had had a chance to view one, so noon found him and Keeper Gallagher eagerly crowded on the curb just opposite the reviewing stand.

Busy street cleaners swept the pavement, souvenir venders hawked their wares, while far down the Avenue they could see the waving of flags and the glinting of brass. Over the roar of the city traffic came the rhythmic thump and blare of approaching bands.

"This looks like a good one," said Keeper Gallagher, "the best since Saint Patrick's a year ago."

At the head of the parade came a rank of Mounted Police. The horses, groomed to perfection, all pranced proudly and danced on polished hooves in time with the music. All, that is, except one, in the exact center of the line. With ears laid back he plodded stolidly along, looking extremely bored and sullen.

Suddenly William Wilmer recognized it as the Policeman's horse to whom he used to give Peppermint Patooties. At the same instant the horse recognized *him*, halted in his tracks and gave a loud whinny. The Policeman, more red-faced than ever, yanked at the reins and spurred viciously, but the horse continued to stand stock still. Still looking at Mr. Wilmer, he calmly sat down. The Policeman leaped off and hauled frantically on the reins, the band halted and marked time, but continued to play, and the other horses milled around excitedly.

Then, after a wink at William Wilmer, the horse slowly lay down in the middle of the Avenue and placidly surveyed the scene.

There was plenty to observe. A Police Inspector and two Captains came galloping up. The Commissioner of Police, the Commissioner of Sewers and Bridges and the Mayor all rushed out from the reviewing stand. The band played the same tune over and over again and the parade was definitely messed up.

"Kelley, get that horse up out of there," roared one of the Captains, "or I'll have your shield off you in two minutes!"

The Policeman, purple now, glared back at the

Captain. "How can I get him up?" he roared back. "Am I a derrick or something?"

The Mayor slammed his broad-brimmed hat on the pavement and stamped on it. "Get an emergency car!" he shrieked. "Get a steam shovel — get a bull-dozer — get an ambulance — get the Fire Department! Get *something! Do* something!"

Mr. Wilmer grasped Keeper Gallagher's arm. "Why, I know him," he exclaimed excitedly. "That's the first horse that ever spoke to me! Maybe I can do something!" — and he started out into the street.

"Hey, come back Mr. Wilmer!" shouted the Keeper. "*Mr. Wilmer!*"

At his cry the reporters in the press box recognized William Wilmer and all began to yell: "Attaboy,

Willie, *you* tell 'im! 'Ray for William Wilmer!" The
sidewalk crowd and the people in the stand now
recognized him and took up the shout. The Mayor
snatched up his hat and glared. "All right, Tarzan,"
he snapped. "Do your stuff and do it fast. Say something! *Do* something!"

William Wilmer squatted down by the horse and
said in his small Animal voice, "Well, good morning.
I haven't seen you in some time. What seems to be
the trouble?"

"No, you haven't," answered the horse, ignoring
his question. "I've missed seeing you. What happened? Lose your job?"

"Well, yes, I did," replied Mr. Wilmer. "But I
have a much nicer one now, up here at the Zoo. I
talk to the animals."

"That sounds fine," said the horse, yawning, "much

more interesting than talking to people. Must be very pleasant. Glad to hear it."

The impatient band struck up a new tune and from all down the Avenue rose the clamor of car horns. The Mayor slammed down his sombrero and stamped on it again. "Come on!" he screamed. "*Say* something! Do something! The whole parade's tied up! The President of Paragunia's tied up!"

"What's ailing *him?*" inquired the horse indolently.

"Well, they want to know what's the matter," said William Wilmer. "You see, it's sort of inconvenient, your lying down here right now."

"It's supposed to be," he replied; "that's why I'm doing it. This is a lie-down strike, on account of Patooties — Patooties and sugar. As you probably know, or perhaps you don't," he explained, "last week some half-witted official gave out an order that no one was to be allowed to feed us horses sugar — or Peppermint Patooties — and you know how fond I am of *them*. You ought to, you've been giving them to me for the past ten years — "

"Eleven years," corrected William Wilmer, "eleven years and about three months."

"Well, ten years or eleven years," the horse went on. "Anyway, I haven't had a Patootie in going on a week now. It's unfair to horses, that's what it is, and you can just tell His Honor the Mayor — and the Commissioner, *and* the President of Paragunia — that

I don't stir from this spot until that order is canceled. And what's more, you can warn them that this movement is going to spread."

Already several of the other horses were showing signs of sitting down, so William Wilmer hastily explained their grievance to the Mayor.

"Who ever gave such a tomfool order?" he screamed. "Who gave that order?" roared the Commissioner, and "Who gave that order?" echoed the Inspector and the two Captains.

"I'm sure *I* don't know," said William Wilmer.

"Well, it's canceled," yelled the Mayor. "Canceled, rescinded, expunged, null and void!"

The Commissioner blew his nose loudly and proclaimed: "From now on all police horses are to be allowed to be fed all the sugar anyone wants to give them — and Peppermint whatever-you-call-ems."

William Wilmer translated this to the horse, who yawned again and then very deliberately rose to his feet. "Good," he said, shaking himself. "Much obliged to you, Mr. Wilmer, and thanks a lot, from all of us. By the way, you haven't a Patootie on you by any chance?"

"Why yes, I have," said Mr. Wilmer, fumbling in his pocket, "I have six."

"Save one for yourself," said the horse, nuzzling up five of them with eager lips, "and thanks again. Hope I'll be seeing you soon."

The Mayor grabbed William Wilmer's arm and hurried him toward the grandstand. "Come on, sit in my box," he ordered; "I want to talk to you."

The crowd cheered even more loudly, the Inspector and the two Captains galloped off, the horses lined up, the Drum Major twirled his baton, the band crashed into a march, and the parade moved on. The Policeman's horse, happily munching his Patooties, arched his neck, and pricked up his ears and strutted with the best of them.

William Wilmer enjoyed the parade very much indeed. He sat between the Mayor and a Navy Admiral, while the Commissioner of Police, who sat behind them, pointed out the various dignitaries in the procession. Of course they asked a good many questions. The Admiral said, "I've been reading about you in the papers, Mr. Wilmer, and all these arguments and theories of the scientists and bishops and politicians and what not, but none of them make much sense. What *I'd* like to know is: Just how do you do it?"

"*I'd* like to know too," William Wilmer answered frankly. "I haven't the faintest idea. I just sort of talk to them and they talk to me, that's all."

The Admiral laughed heartily and clapped him on the shoulder. "Well, that's the first honest and sensible explanation of your great talent that I've heard yet. '*You just sort of talk to them and they talk to you.*'

By George, it's refreshing to meet an honest and simple man. Any time you'd like to visit a battleship, just let me know. Be delighted to have you."

The Mayor suddenly questioned, "Wilmer, just what in thunder *is* a Peppermint what-do-you-call-it?"

"Patootie?" answered William Wilmer. "Why — I think I have one here" — and he offered his remaining Patootie. The Policeman's horse had snuffled on it some and it was a bit gray from his pocket, but the Mayor sucked it with apparent pleasure. "Why, that's excellent," he said, "quite delicious. That horse had good sense. Horse sense. Ha, ha, ha!" No one else laughed so he went on more seriously: —

"Now listen, Wilmer. We've had considerable trouble in the Mounted Police because of horses who don't get on with their riders and riders who don't get on with their horses. If you could act as Liaison Officer — you know: have a little chat with them every few months, iron out their misunderstandings and so on — I'm sure it would improve the efficiency of the Mounted Division by 150 per cent. What do you say?"

"Why that would be very nice," he answered. "I'd be delighted to — "

"Fine!" interrupted the Mayor. "That's settled." He fished in his pocket and brought out a large gold badge which he pinned on William Wilmer's coat. "There now, you're officially appointed a Special

Deputy Commissioner of Police. It's honorary, of course, there's no salary attached."

"That's fine," said William Wilmer, "I have so many salaries and retainers and things now that I can't keep track of them. Thank you very much."

"Don't mention it," said the Mayor heartily. "Come down and have lunch with me at City Hall next Monday. I only have crackers and a glass of milk though."

"That's all right, I usually only have a glass of milk," William Wilmer answered.

The parade went on for at least two hours. Band after band passed. There were flags and soldiers and sailors, political and religious societies, bridge clubs, Girl Scouts and Boy Scouts, tanks, cannon, jeeps and street-cleaning equipment. The President of Paragunia arrived, was welcomed by the Mayor and the Governor and took his place between them in the official reviewing box. He smiled pleasantly at everyone and everything, but as he didn't speak any English and no one present spoke Paragunian the conversation was quite limited.

The Admiral nudged William Wilmer and chuckled, "Maybe you could do something with him, Wilmer, I understand you're a great hand with crocodiles."

On the opposite curb Keeper Gallagher murmured: "Glory be, and isn't he the great lad? Only last Saturday coming into the Lion House and talking with

Toby — and me thinking he was nuts; and now him hobnobbing with Mayors and Admirals and Presidents of Paragunia and all. And just as easy and pleasant as if he was talking with me or Lucy or the Director himself."

The afternoon was far gone when William Wilmer got back to his quiet office. On his coat gleamed the gold badge of a Deputy Commissioner, he was lunching at City Hall on Monday, he had a cordial invitation to visit the Admiral's flagship at any time — and in his pocket was the calling card of the President of Paragunia. He should have been very happy, but he was not. In fact, he was becoming quite worried.

For it was now Wednesday afternoon; he had had his new job for almost three whole days and seemed to have accomplished nothing. He had answered only a few of the letters to the zoos, he wrote so slowly and so many other things had been happening. Now there were three more shoe boxes of letters and telegrams to be gone over. He hadn't even begun on his series of magazine articles.

What was still worse, except for the one short interview with the black panther, he had done nothing to justify his position at the Zoo — he had scarcely had time even to speak to Lucy or Toby.

He had signed dozens of contracts and testimonials, but hardly knew what he had signed or where they were. Checks had been arriving in every mail and he had put them all in the cigar box in his bureau drawer. He didn't quite know what to do with them, for he had never had a bank account. He hadn't even added them up, but the box was almost full, there must be a lot of money there. In the meantime he had been living on last week's envelope. That was about gone now and he had still forgotten to pay Mrs. Keeler his board money.

As usual, he took his worries to Director Carrington-Carr. First, however, he had to explain the gold badge.

"My, my," laughed the Director, "you certainly *are* stepping out, William. His Honor the Mayor and Admiral Canary you say, *and* the President of Paragunia. Watch your step, my boy, or they'll be making you an Ambassador or something. Well, I've always wanted to know a policeman and now I have one for a pal — and a Commissioner, no less! Next time I get arrested for speeding I'll call on you — "

But William Wilmer was too worried to enjoy pleasantries, and plunged into a recital of his troubles. When he had finished the Director said, "Why it's perfectly simple, William, what you need is a private secretary."

Mr. Wilmer, thinking he was still joking, smiled sadly, but the Director went on: "I'm perfectly serious. Why, look — here you've been laboring for three days trying to write those few zoo letters, and you've barely made a start on them. A good secretary could have cleaned them all up in a couple of hours. And think of your articles for Pulpwood; why, you'd be a month apiece on them at the rate you write! But a good secretary could take them down in shorthand as fast as you or Lucy could talk, and type them — and put in all the commas — in no time. And your telephone calls and mail; a good secretary will take care of those, arrange your engagements, file your contracts — "

"But goodness — a secretary — *me* with a secretary!" gasped Mr. Wilmer. "Why, only Big Executives have secretaries — besides I couldn't afford it."

"How much have you in the bank — right now?" interrupted the Director.

"Why — er — nothing," said William Wilmer. "You see, I've never had a bank account. I've put all the checks that have come in in that cigar box in my bureau drawer. I guess they amount to quite a lot, but I don't know, I haven't added them up."

"Good Lord," murmured the Director. "Perhaps I'm wrong. Maybe we ought to get a nurse, instead of a secretary. . . .

"Now then — suppose that tomorrow morning you gather up your cigar box of checks and bring it over here — and don't leave it on the bus. We might count them up, just for the fun of it, and then we'll go over to the Wheat Exchange Bank and start you an account. *Then* we'll set about getting you a secretary — unless you have someone in mind."

William Wilmer gulped and turned red, then recklessly burst out, "Well, there *was* a young lady at the Safe, Sane and Colossal Company, a Miss Sweeney — she was a secretary, she took dictation and typed awfully fast and — "

"And was not entirely unattractive?" smiled Mr. Carrington-Carr.

"She was very nice," William Wilmer hurried on. "She has red hair and when I was fired she said she wished *she* was out of that jail, so maybe she would consider leaving — "

"Fine," said the Director, rising. "Now tomorrow morning, after we have visited the bank, you will don your shining golden badge, and armed with a brand-new checkbook and your trusty fountain pen (I hope you *have* a fountain pen) you will mount a mettle-some taxicab and storm the castle of that nasty Mr. Switch or Twitch, or whatever his name is. You will rescue the beautiful auburn-haired Princess and bring her safely to the sanctuary of our peaceful Zoo — and I hope she doesn't chew gum."

"She doesn't — ever," said Mr. Wilmer.

"Good," said the Director. "Now get yourself home, William, and get a good night's sleep, for great deeds are toward. And try to stop worrying so con-foundedly."

"Thank you," said William Wilmer. "Thanks ever so much."

CHAPTER VI

Inefficiency Expert

WILLIAM WILMER
managed to get his cigar box of checks safely to the
office next morning. He wore his tannish gray suit,
which was most becoming, and a new necktie. He
didn't quite know what to do about the gold Commissioner's badge, he supposed he ought to wear it,
but it looked very conspicuous on his coat, so he
pinned it on his vest, well out of sight.

The Director, who helped him add up the checks,
gave a startled exclamation when he arrived at the
total. "Well, William," he smiled. "Do you know
what you're worth at the moment? Fifty-two thousand, seven hundred and fifty!"

"Dollars?" gasped William Wilmer.

"No. Salted peanuts," answered Mr. Carrington-
Carr. "Come, let's get this in the bank, it makes me

nervous. You're likely to feed it to the hippopotamus or something."

William Wilmer was introduced to a vice president of the bank, who was most cordial. He invited them into his office and they chatted there while a clerk made out the necessary forms, showed him where to sign them, presented him with a neat deposit book and a small folding checkbook.

The Vice President also showed him how to make out a check, which was a totally new experience for William Wilmer.

"I — er — wonder," he inquired hesitantly, "if I could get out a little real money for myself. You see, I have only about three dollars and forty cents left and I owe Mrs. Keeler for last week's board."

The others enjoyed a hearty laugh and showed him how to make out a check to "Cash." The clerk hastened away with it and, returning, handed him a hundred dollars in crisp new bills.

"See how easy it is?" laughed the Director. "Much *too* easy. Don't make a habit of it." Then, rising, he said: "Come now, Lochinvar, gird yourself for the fray. Go beard your Twitch in his dismal lair and don't you dare return without the beautiful Princess. Yoicks, tallyho, and all that."

William Wilmer went down in the subway. At the station he bought his copy of the *Daily Bleat* and a roll of Peppermint Patooties. The front page of the paper of course was filled with pictures of yesterday's parade, and of him and the Policeman's horse, of the horse lying down and the horse getting up, of the Mayor and Admiral Canary and the President of Paragunia chatting with him. There were accounts of his appointment as a Deputy Commissioner and even a picture of the gold badge.

It all should have been very exciting, but as the train roared along a terrible feeling of gloom descended on William Wilmer. It just did not seem possible that the events of the past week could have happened. Here he was in the same subway, going down to the same Safe, Sane and Colossal office. He would be late and Mr. Twitch would be unpleasant. He would be the same Mr. Wilmer, pounding the keys of that hateful adding machine through all the rest of his dreary days.

Vainly he looked down at his beautiful new tweeds, he slipped his hand under his coat and touched the gold badge. He reached in his inside pocket and felt his well-filled wallet. He took out his deposit book and tried to reassure himself by the neat figures just entered in it — $52,750 — but it was all no use: the gloom only deepened.

His spirits lifted slightly when, walking the old familiar route, he approached the Policeman's horse. The horse recognized him from a distance and eagerly pawed the curb. The Policeman recognized him, too,

and snapped to a rigid salute.

"*Good* morning sir," he said pleasantly. "A lovely morning!"

Mr. Wilmer hadn't noticed the morning especially.

"I'd like to congratulate you, sir, on your appointment," the Policeman went on. "It's a fine idea, even if it was the Mayor's. Dick here has been a different horse since yesterday."

"Oh, thanks," said William Wilmer, fumbling in his pocket. "Is it all right if I give him a Patootie?"

"Of course, of course," the Policeman replied genially. "That ruling has been rescinded, thanks to you; and I'd like to apologize, sir, for being tough about it last week — but orders is orders, you know."

"Orders nothing," chuckled the horse, nuzzling up a whole handful of Patooties. "It was indigestion — indigestion and bad temper. But everything's all pie and cake now; you can't imagine the change that's come over these cops since yesterday. All of them scared to death about what their horses may tell on them. I might add that you're about the most popular Commissioner who's ever been appointed to the Force — among the horses anyway."

"Thanks," said William Wilmer absently, "that's fine." He returned the Policeman's salute, rather awkwardly, and continued on his way.

As he approached the S. S. & C. Building, the feeling of depression settled down even more heavily. He saw hundreds of clerks hurrying through the revolving doors that seemed like great ravenous funnels sucking people in. They reminded him of the gutter drains down which the water flooded in a rainstorm — water carrying bits of paper and fallen leaves. They floated so jauntily, until suddenly they were sucked down into the darkness. He felt like a leaf or a chewing gum wrapper being swept toward the hungry gratings.

He had a terrified feeling that if he got close enough those doors would suck him in. His lovely new clothes would vanish, his bank account would disappear. His pleasant office, Toby, Lucy, Mr. Gallagher and the

Director would only be memories. Already he thought he could again smell the odor of the office — the sourish smell of hundreds of typewriter ribbons, of erasers and rubberized covers. Again he could almost hear the incessant clatter of the adding machines, the unpleasant rasp of Mr. Twitch's voice.

"Oh dear, I just can't face it," he groaned. "I just *can't*."

Hastily he crossed the street and passed on the far side, keeping his eyes turned from those horrible sucking doors. As he turned into the Avenue he found that he was drenched with sweat and little creepy prickles were running up the back of his neck. He felt a great relief, but he felt terribly ashamed and completely futile. "I guess I'm just not much of a Lochinvar," he had to admit.

He suddenly became aware of a flowershop, and Mrs. Keeler's words came back to him: "The way to a woman's heart is with flowers."

It was a very expensive-looking flowershop. There was a doorman, much more elaborately uniformed than Admiral Canary. There were newly watered window boxes, gay with brightly blossomed plants; the windows looked like conservatories. Summoning what courage he had left, and making sure he hadn't lost his wallet, William Wilmer went in.

The clerk who languidly approached seemed even more formidable than Mr. Twitch. Again reaching for his wallet William Wilmer inadvertently exposed the gold badge. The clerk's attitude at once became disgustingly subservient. "And what would it be today sir?" he inquired.

"I'd — er — like to get some — flowers, if you're not too busy," said William Wilmer. "Some — er — flowers."

"Oh yes, yes, something for a young lady, I presume," smirked the clerk. "Something in the way of a corsage? We have some superb new orchids. We could do something really stunning with them, actually heart-lifting, something, say, at about twenty-five dollars?"

William Wilmer gulped slightly, recollecting that that was almost his former weekly wage. Then, suddenly inspired, he said, "No. Make it thirty-four eighty-six — less bond payments, Withholding Tax and Social Security."

"Yes, indeed sir," said the slightly puzzled clerk. "And now was there something else?"

"Yes," said William Wilmer. "I'd like something for my landlady, Mrs. Keeler. She's sort of middle-aged."

"Oh yes, the old-fashioned-garden type," said the clerk. "Moss roses perhaps, iris, jonquils, pansies, violets; something at about ten dollars?"

"Make it twenty," he decided recklessly, "and put in a couple of gardenias for Mr. Keeler."

The clerk showed him to an alcove where there was a desk with cards, envelopes and notepaper. He just signed his name to a card for Mrs. Keeler, but for Miss Sweeney he selected a sheet of notepaper. The shop was almost empty, so he was able to concentrate, and eventually managed to write: —

My dear Miss Sweeney: —

Director Carrington-Carr says that I must get a secretary and I guess he is right, because everything is in a terrible mess. I was wondering if you would possibly consider taking the position? I know it is impertinent of me to ask, but I really need help very much. The office is very pleasant and everyone is awfully nice.

I went to the S. S. & C. office to ask you about it personally, but I was afraid to go in. I wonder if you would be kind enough to communicate with me about it?

Yours truly,
WILLIAM WILMER

After he had given the cards to the clerk and paid the bill he felt a little better. At least he had done *something* about getting a secretary; but still, he was glad that the Director was out of town for the rest of the day. He boarded a bus and hastened up to the Zoo, resolved to work hard on his correspondence and to try to get some of it straightened out.

However, the moment he arrived there Keeper Gallagher nodded toward the office and said, "Three gents to see you."

The smallest and least impressive of the three introduced himself as Mr. Wentworth Pringle, President of the Peppermint Patooties Corporation. The second was his production manager, and the third was a Mr. Blither, of the Bunk, Blither and Blither Advertising Agency. He wore a double-breasted suit and reminded William Wilmer somewhat of Mr. Twitch.

"Mr. Wilmer," the President began, "that stunt of yours with the horse in the parade yesterday was the most stupendous advertising idea ever conceived and put over in the history of the Patooties Corporation. Do you realize that since yesterday noon the sale of Peppermint Patooties has jumped over 800 per cent in the Metropolitan district alone? We are already planning the addition of a new wing which will double the capacity of our factory. We are also pre-paring a nation-wide advertising campaign based on yesterday's incident. Show him the layouts, Blither."

Mr. Blither spread out a lot of pencil sketches which didn't look like anything much to William Wilmer, so he didn't say anything. "There will be a series of ten," the President went on, "and we would like your endorsement of them. What would be your price?"

"Er — five thousand dollars, I think," said William Wilmer.

"*Each?*" asked the President.

"Why yes, I guess so," he replied, wishing that he could get at his letter writing.

The President whistled slightly. "That makes fifty thousand for the series," he said, "couldn't you shade that figure a trifle, Mr. Wilmer?"

William Wilmer didn't know what "shading a figure" meant, he thought it was something that artists did, so he said he guessed he couldn't.

"O.K.," agreed Mr. Pringle. "Five thousand per. Now Mr. Wilmer, we would also like to have you appear on the Peppermint Patooties Parade. As you probably know, it is broadcast every Friday evening at 9:15 over a national hook-up; you would be on for three minutes, forty seconds."

"Oh goodness, I couldn't do that," protested William Wilmer. "I couldn't go on the radio. I can't croon or anything."

"You wouldn't have to," interrupted Mr. Blither. "Everything will be written out, you'll just read it. We might arrange to have you interview some animals too — that would be sensational, can't you visualize it?"

"No, I can't," said William Wilmer, "because when I talk with animals no one else can hear us. I don't think that would be very sensational."

"Oh, we'll hire voices," Mr. Blither assured him. "There's Letty O'Gargle, she can do any sort of animal, and Charlie McNasty, he could do you perfectly."

"But that doesn't seem quite honest," objected William Wilmer.

"I wouldn't know about that," answered Mr. Blither impatiently, "but it's good advertising. What would be your price, Mr. Wilmer, for say ten appearances?"

"Oh, five thousand, I suppose," he answered wearily, "each."

They all began to talk at once about contracts and conferences and options, but William Wilmer, whose head was beginning to ache, rose and, in a manner as much like the Director's as he could manage, announced, "I am sorry, gentlemen, but you will have to arrange all these details with my secretary. I have an appointment right now — with a rhinoceros."

"Where *is* your secretary?" they demanded. "When can she be seen?"

"I don't know," he sighed, "I haven't got one yet."

As the trio left the building they were arguing heatedly. "He's nuts, I tell you," said the Production Manager, "plain nuts."

"Not at all," said Mr. Blither. "He's a genius and you just don't understand geniuses, as we in the advertising profession do."

"I'm glad there's *something* you understand," grunted President Pringle. "So far this bright little idea of yours promises to cost us exactly one hundred thousand bucks. I hope it's worth it."

William Wilmer worked hard at his letter writing all the rest of the day, but by evening he had only accomplished about six letters and there were still two full shoe boxes to be answered.

"Oh, dear," he said helplessly, "I guess I'm a failure at letter writing too. I'm just not getting anywhere."

On the way home he stopped to have a chat with Lucy. She was complaining of foot trouble. "It's always like this in the spring, Mr. Wilmer," she said. "It's the warm weather I suppose, and this hard concrete. Why they have these hard concrete floors, I just can't imagine; they just *kill* my feet. If I could only get them in a nice squidgy mud hole, or in a nice cool stream. If I could only walk around in a nice soft green meadow or roll in some long sweet grass, I'd be a different elephant. I really don't like city life, Mr. Wilmer, do you?"

"Well, I don't know," he said. "When I was little I used to go to my uncle's farm and it certainly was nice to get your shoes and stockings off and squidge your feet in the mud. I remember there was a spring under a willow tree. The water was so clear that you hardly knew it was there and so cold that it made your feet feel numb when you put them in it. There were lots of little bright green frogs and the ground all around was soft and muddy and — "

"Stop, Mr. Wilmer, or you'll have me crying," cried Lucy plaintively.

"I'll ask Mr. Carrington-Carr if he can't arrange something in the way of a pool for you," he promised. "I'm sure he can."

"Thanks ever so much, Mr. Wilmer, even a little mud puddle would be some help."

He went home worried and depressed. All his affairs seemed to be in such confusion. There were so many interruptions; he never had time to get anything done. Worse still was the thought of facing

Director Carrington-Carr in the morning, of admitting that he had not even seen Miss Sweeney, that he had lacked the courage to enter the S. S. & C. Building. The Director had been so kind and so thoughtful; William Wilmer hated to prove such a disappointment.

He found Mrs. Keeler in gala array. She was wearing her best black silk dress and her bosom was adorned with the most beautiful corsage he had ever beheld. It was mostly rare orchids, with other flowers that he didn't know the names of, and there were slender dangling ribbons of pure white silk.

His heart sank at the sight. "Good Heavens," he thought. "Those are Miss Sweeney's flowers! I must have mixed up the cards, or the addresses or something. And *she* has the old-fashioned-garden flowers suitable for an elderly lady. *Now* what will she think of me? I wonder what else I can do wrong today?"

Mrs. Keeler was very festive during dinner and Mr. Keeler entered gladly into the spirit. "Willie, you're certainly demoralizing the old lady," he laughed. "Wants to go to the movies again tonight, and her looking like a walking conservatory. Better come along and help me drive away the glamor boys."

"Yes, do come, Mr. Wilmer," she urged. "Imagine wearing orchids and stepping out with *that!*"

But William Wilmer was too occupied in wondering whether Miss Sweeney would be insulted by his gift of old-fashioned flowers, whether she would answer his note and what the Director would say in the morning. He excused himself on the ground of sleepiness and climbed up to his room. Removing his wallet from his coat he was reminded that he *still* hadn't paid Mrs. Keeler for last week's board.

"Well I guess Mr. Carrington-Carr was right," he said ruefully. "I don't need a secretary, what I need is a nurse — or a Keeper. I wonder if Mr. Gallagher would take the job."

Hearts and Flowers

WILLIAM WILMER
wrote busily at his letters, dreading the moment when
the Director would demand to know what he had
done about getting a secretary. It was almost eleven
and he had only accomplished two, when the door
opened and Mr. Carrington-Carr strode in. "Good
morning, William," he said, glancing about. "Where
is the beautiful Princess?"

William Wilmer blushed and writhed and stammered as he tried to explain his dread of the S. S. & C.
Building, his failure to enter it and his inefficient
flower buying. "I *did* send her a note," he finished
lamely. The Director withered him with an accusing
glance.

"*You sent her a note!*" he cried. "A fine knight
errant you are! A peerless Galahad! You, a Deputy

Police Commissioner, afraid to enter an office building; terrified of a Twitch! You sent her a note — Bah!
A note and a nosegay, and the wrong one at that! . . .

"Do you know what I'm going to do?" he roared,
pacing up and down. "*I'm* going to get you a secretary.
I'm going to get you the secretary that you deserve.
She's going to be an old maid in her late sixties. She's
going to be tall and angular, with a long thin red nose
and spectacles. She's going to have a disposition like
the black panther and a voice like a rusty file. She's — "

His tirade was interrupted by the intrusion of
Keeper Gallagher's head in the side doorway. "Lady
to see Mr. Wilmer," he announced.

The outside sun burnished her coppery hair with
a glowing sheen. She wore a funny little hat and on

her dark blue jacket glowed two gardenias that seemed to fill the room with their perfume.

"Hello," she smiled, crossing the office and extending her hand to William Wilmer. "Here I am." Then, turning to the Director, her nose wrinkling in that entrancing way, "And I imagine this is Director Carrington-Carr, isn't it?"

"It *was*," he replied. "It was, but now it is just a poor, stunned creature, marveling at the blind way Fortune tosses her favors about. What has *he* ever done to deserve all this — the incompetent, fumbling, cowardly, note-writing poltroon?" He grinned kindly as he shook hands. "If he wasn't such a nice guy I could hate him."

"But — er — Miss Sweeney," Mr. Wilmer gasped, "are you really considering the job — I mean position?"

"Considering it?" she smiled. "Why, I've accepted it. I accepted it yesterday, about five minutes after your note came. If I'd realized what a lovely office it was I wouldn't have hesitated that long."

"Did you give Mr. Twitch notice?" he asked, still slightly dazed.

"Yes, fifteen minutes'."

"From the impression I have gathered of your Mr. Twitch," laughed the Director, "fifteen minutes was overgenerous."

"No, it was just right," she grinned. "I needed

exactly twelve minutes to tell him what I thought of him, and three to get my hat and coat — and flowers."

"I don't suppose," inquired Mr. Carrington-Carr, "that our young note-writing friend here thought to mention any trivial little details such as hours, duties or salary?"

"Why no. I — er — " began William Wilmer.

"Well, do it now," he said, entering his own office. "BUT," he called back, "the salary must be exactly double what Mr. Switch bestowed; I insist on that."

"It's *Twitch*," William Wilmer began, "not Switch — " but the Director, muttering "Oh Lord," slammed the door.

William Wilmer offered Miss Sweeney a chair and tried to disguise his relief and happiness by being very businesslike.

"Now the — er — hours," he began, "are — er — well I don't exactly know, just whatever you need to get things sort of done. The — er — duties are, well you know, typewriting and things, and the salary, of course, will be twice what the S. S. & C. Company paid, just as Mr. Carrington-Carr said. I don't know just what your salary was there, but — "

Miss Sweeney, who had been watching a humming-bird hovering over the syringa outside the window, suddenly turned and said, "Oh, I'm sorry — I wasn't listening. It's all right I'm sure. But what I *really* want to know is about the flowers.

"How did you *know* that I loved old-fashioned flowers? How did you know that moss roses were my special favorites? Grandmother used to have them in her garden at home. And the jonquils and pansies, violets and sweet peas. And two gardenias to wear — they're the only hot-house flowers I've ever liked.

"It was the flowers, really, that decided me on this job. If you had sent the usual, expensive corsage — orchids and that sort of thing (I loathe orchids) — I think I would still be at the S. S. & C. office, Twitch and all."

William Wilmer breathed a great sigh of relief. He felt that in honesty he really should explain that it was all a mistake; that it was his ineptness and not his understanding that had sent her Mrs. Keeler's old-fashioned flowers; but before he could speak the Director popped his head in and called: "If you two have fought out your terms you might join me in a bite to eat. Gallagher has been foraging at the Park restaurant; I can't guarantee the results, but it looks like food and it smells like food, so let's try."

It was the happiest luncheon William Wilmer had ever experienced. Keeper Gallagher's efforts seemed wonderfully successful to him, but then, he wouldn't have known whether he was eating soup, eggs or alligator food. Mr. Carrington-Carr and Miss Sweeney laughed and chatted, he even made a few fairly successful attempts himself. But mostly he just gazed at the gardenias on Miss Sweeney's jacket. He thought how much more becoming they were there than they would have been on Mr. Keeler's lapel and thanked his lucky star for his fortunate inefficiency.

Eventually the Director, rising, said, "Well, children, much as I regret leaving this pleasant gathering, I must get up to East Westchester or West Eastchester or some place and lecture to the Ladies' Nature Club, on how to tell the birds from the animals. I'm glad you've come Miss Sweeney, I hope you'll be happy here, I'm pretty sure you will. And if you can straighten out that combination Gordian Knot and Augean Stables that Young Lochinvar here has accumulated on his desk, you're even more wonderful than I think you are."

"Thank you," she replied, her nose crinkling, "I'll do my best."

William Wilmer explained to her, or tried to, about the zoo letters and what he had done and hadn't done, mostly the latter. He showed her the stacks of contracts and endorsements, agreements and offers. He showed her the filing cabinet, his stationery and the typewriter, which he had never attempted to use.

"I see," she said, hanging up her jacket. "Now why don't you just go out and talk to some of your animal friends, while I get to work on this? It's a lovely afternoon. You might tell Lucy that I'm dying to meet her

and shall, as soon as I get things straightened out —
and give my best to Toby." She flicked a few bread-
crumbs from his bluish gray tweed coat. "And thanks
for the flowers — they meant a lot."

He spent the pleasantest and most useful afternoon
since he had been there. In company with Keeper
Gallagher he wandered about the Zoo chatting with
all the animals, many of whom he had not yet met.

There were a few complaints, none of them serious.
The horned toads said that their sand was too damp
and cold. One of the hyenas protested that their meat
was much too fresh. A boa constrictor mentioned a
pain in the throat, which he felt sure was caused by
a chicken bone. William Wilmer made careful notes
of all these troubles and promised to call them to the
Director's attention.

Lucy was still having foot trouble, but was greatly
pleased when he told her about the animal interviews
that he was to write and informed her that she was
to be the subject of the first one.

"My, my, think of that," she said. "That's very thrilling Mr. Wilmer, and in the *Post Companion!* I'll feel like a movie star or something. I certainly must think up some favorite Burmese recipes, they like that sort of thing, don't they?"

"I guess so," answered William Wilmer. "And you'll have your portrait painted by Mr. Bullington Livingston, the famous animal artist."

"Why that's just wonderful," she giggled, "but I *must* get a good mud pack and have my toenails really presentable, just some crude oil and a little sandpapering, you know, and perhaps a bit of whitewash."

"I'll tell Keeper Gallagher," he promised, writing it all down. "I'm sure he'll be glad to take care of that."

Toby seemed most contented. He had just had his first solid meal and was busy washing up. "That meat certainly hit the spot, Mr. Wilmer," he purred. "Gruel and stuff is all right, but a fellow does crave something solid to get his teeth into, what teeth he has left. It's healing fine though, and I'm to be on real meat from now on."

"How would you like to be on the radio, Toby?" he inquired. "I've sort of promised to interview some of you folks on the Patooties Parade and I'd like you to be the first, if you don't mind."

"Why, I'd like it fine," answered Toby. "Wonder if I could get a nip off one of those crooners or those moaning girls. Sound like they'd be pretty tender eating."

"I doubt it," laughed William Wilmer, "they'd probably make you sick; they do me and I've never had so much as a nibble of one."

Late afternoon came almost before he realized it. It had been such a pleasant few hours, and William Wilmer felt thoroughly happy and unworried. At last he had managed really to accomplish something. That chicken bone in the boa constrictor's throat must be very painful, the horned toads were quite unhappy and there was a bear who thought he had a splinter in his paw. The black panther was sleeping well in her new cage, her disposition had improved wonderfully. Yes, he was really earning his salary now.

When he entered the office Miss Sweeney was seated in a big chair gazing at the view from the window. The air was heavy with lilacs and mock orange. The low sun threw long dark shadows across the brilliant green lawns. Down on the lake the sails of toy boats glowed warm in the golden light, children's voices sounded far off. Birds twittered and fussed over the evening meal.

"Isn't it beautiful?" William Wilmer said.

"It's the most beautiful office in the world," she answered, still looking out. "To think of being paid to work here!"

"It does seem silly doesn't it?" he agreed. "And to think that less than a week ago I was working at that awful S. S. & C. office and never dreamed that such a place as this existed."

Miss Sweeney gave a slight shudder. "Don't speak of it," she said, "I was there until yesterday, I haven't quite had time to realize that all this is real. Did you have a good afternoon?"

"Wonderful," he answered. "It's the first time since I came here that I've really accomplished anything. I got a lot done."

"That's good," she smiled, finally tearing her gaze from the green outdoors. "I did pretty well myself."

William Wilmer glanced at the desk and his jaw dropped in astonishment. Gone were all the disorderly piles of papers, the shoe boxes, the scattered telegrams. On the newly dusted surface were only a vase of blossoms and a stack of neatly addressed and stamped envelopes.

"Those are your zoo letters," she said. "They're all finished. I've filed and listed all the contracts and agreements and offers. There are a few that I'll have to ask you about later, but everything's pretty well under control. I hope Mr. Carrington-Carr won't skin me for cutting a few blossoms. I know it's against the Park rules, but I just couldn't resist them."

"I don't think he'd mind anything you do," smiled William Wilmer.

"He's a dear, isn't he?" she said.

"He's the nicest man I've ever known," William Wilmer said. "I only wish I could be more like him."

"You've done pretty well in six days," she grinned impishly, "the clothes especially, they certainly make a difference. Well," she added, rising and putting on the funny little hat, "I guess we might as well call it a day."

"Can I — that is — could I see you — er — take you — Where do you live?" he floundered.

She was adjusting the hat in the mirror and spoke casually over her shoulder, "Why, at Mrs. Keeler's."

"Mrs. Keeler's!" he gasped. "You — how — er — you mean Mrs. Keeler's?"

She nodded. "Yes, I thought it would be more convenient, near the Park and everything. I used to live way down town; it would have been an awful trip every day. And then if I was going to be your secretary it seemed sensible to be at the same place, you might want to do some of your work at home. So — bright and early this morning I took myself up to Mrs. Keeler's, engaged a room — she's a dear, isn't she? — and moved in, bag, baggage, typewriter, flowers and — Eleanor."

"Eleanor?" he queried weakly.

"Yes, my canary, you know. He sings beautifully."

"Eleanor . . . *He* sings . . ." Mrs. Keeler . . . !

It was all too much for William Wilmer. In a daze he

found his new hat, put it on — backwards — and followed her out into the Park.

Keeper Gallagher reined in his mettlesome jalopy
and called, "You folks are going my way aren't you?
How about a lift?"

"Oh, fine," cried Miss Sweeney, scrambling into the
front seat, while William Wilmer climbed into the
back. "Why, this is *wonderful*, Mr. Gallagher, traveling home in real style!"

Inspired by the appreciation, Keeper Gallagher
put the old car through its paces and they rattled up
through the Park at an exhilarating speed. Miss
Sweeney snatched off the funny little hat and, turning, called through the blowing mass of her coppery
hair: "Isn't it *wonderful*, Mr. Wilmer?"

"Yes indeed," he laughed, clutching his hat as they swooped around a curve, "everything's wonderful, today."

At home Mr. Keeler displayed an almost alarming appearance of dressiness. His Sunday suit was newly pressed, his shoes shined dazzlingly. His hair was roached up and his walrus mustache trimmed and curled.

"Good evening, Willie," he cried festively, "*and* Miss Sweeney." He made a deep bow. "That express-man brought your books and things, I've put them all up in your room."

"You've certainly been a wonderful influence, Miss Sweeney," beamed Mrs. Keeler. "Why, you wouldn't believe the energy he's had today! Carried up your things, washed the windows, swept the rugs and look at him now — dressed up like a debutante. And as for Eleanor, he's been singing like an angel the whole day. It certainly makes things homelike. There's nothing I love like a canary singing — except orchids." She caressed the elaborate corsage which she had managed to nurse through the day. "You certainly are spoiling me, Mr. Wilmer. It's the movies again to-night. As long as I have an orchid on me I've got to be going places."

After dinner Mr. Wilmer agreed to accompany the Keelers to the movies, but Miss Sweeney begged off. "It's been a pretty full day," she explained, "mov-

ing, a new job, a new home, and I've not half unpacked
yet. You're dears to ask me though." She ran lightly
upstairs, but a moment later leaned over the railing
and tossed a gardenia down to Mr. Keeler. "For your
buttonhole," she called. "Thank you so much for all
you've done, Mr. Keeler, you're just *wonderful*."

Mrs. Keeler could scarcely wait to clear the door
before sounding the praises of Miss Sweeney. "A perfect lamb, Mr. Wilmer, a sweet lamb, that's what she
is. So pleasant and so stylish-dressed and so beautiful.
Don't you think she's beautiful, Mr. Wilmer?"

"Why — er — I guess so," answered William Wilmer. "I — hadn't thought."

"And her hair," she went on ecstatically. "What
hair! Like polished copper it is, and that thick. It
reminds me a little of my hair when I was a girl, back
in Lynn, Massachusetts."

"It doesn't me," said Mr. Keeler, strutting along
with his hat cocked at a jaunty angle, "not in the
least."

William Wilmer caught her arm, saying hastily,
"Oh no, Mrs. Keeler, I wouldn't — not here — it's
such a pleasant evening."

CHAPTER VIII

Engagement Calendar

NOW BEGAN the happiest, most contented period of William Wilmer's life, thus far. Within two days Miss Sweeney had all his affairs in perfect order. She answered his letters, she filed his contracts, she tended the telephone and guarded him from the reporters, curiosity seekers and autograph hunters. She saw the Peppermint Patooties trio, signed their contracts and sent them away contented and much impressed.

She purchased an engagement book in which she neatly wrote down all his appointments. She took charge of his bank account, paid Mrs. Keeler and herself and gave him spending money whenever he wanted it, which was not very often.

Best of all, she managed to do all this without ever seeming officious or bossy. She never hurried, she never stamped around, she never rattled things and she never used the typewriter except when he was out. Whenever he came into the office he usually found her sitting in one of the large chairs looking out at the lake, knitting or arranging flowers. She loved to arrange flowers.

Keeper Gallagher, like everyone else, had become her eager slave. Being an intimate of all the Park gardeners and hence a privileged character, he appeared at the office door each morning bearing an armful of flowers or blossoms. "Of course it's against Park rules to cut anything," he always grinned, "but the plants and shrubs *do* need thinning and pruning and it would be a shame to be throwing these away."

She always received them with exclamations of joy and always said, "Oh thank you Mr. Gallagher, you're just *won*derful!"

William Wilmer soon observed that the way she opened her dark blue eyes very wide and breathed, "Oh . . . you're just *won*derful!" was one of the

most effective forms of bribery in the world. It wrought amazing results on everyone from the Director to the black panther. It had made a new man of Mr. Keeler, his energy was alarming, his dressiness dazzling. He even got a job — and kept it.

All this gave William Wilmer complete freedom to do his real work. At once he decided to have a personal chat with every animal in the Zoo. In less than a day he interviewed the entire population of the Large Mammal House, making notes on their personal histories, their likes and dislikes and their complaints.

In an incredibly short time Miss Sweeney typed all his notes, correctly spelled and with the commas in the right places, and bound them in a neat folder. It was a proud moment for William Wilmer when he laid his effort on the Director's desk. Mr. Carrington-Carr read it through carefully and when he finally spoke it was without any of his usual bantering air.

"William," he said, "this survey, when finished, will be one of the greatest forward steps ever taken in the study of Natural History. Never, since animals were first caged, and that's several hundred years ago, have we known just how they felt about things, what their thoughts and problems were. Now we shall know exactly, from their own lips.

"When you have surveyed all the other zoos in the country you will have made a most tremendous contribution to the welfare and contentment of all captive animals. It is a fine and worthwhile task and you have made a splendid start on it."

"Thank you very much," said William Wilmer, glowing with pride, "I want to get at the snakes tomorrow."

One of the first entries in the new engagement book was his appointment with Frou-Frou and Mrs. Plushington on Sunday evening at nine. The big blue car arrived for him promptly at eight forty-five, occasioning considerable heavy-handed jocularity on Mr. Keeler's part about the girl friend at the Giltdorf Towers.

"He's just jealous," observed Mrs. Keeler, "because he can't get a ride in that car."

"Why don't you take him along?" suggested Miss Sweeney. "I'm sure Mrs. Plushington wouldn't mind."

"The chauffeur might," William Wilmer hesitated.

"Oh no," she grinned. "Just tell him it's your old grandfather, in need of an airing."

They left amid gales of laughter from Mrs. Keeler; the chauffeur did not object in the least, so Mr. Keeler lit a cigar and lolled back on the pale blue cushions with great contentment.

"Don't hurry, Willie," he said, when they had reached their destination, "I'll wait here and have a chat with the boys." He passed out cigars to the chauffeur and footman, who seemed slightly startled but accepted them with thanks.

The tête-à-tête was much less painful than William Wilmer had expected. Frou-Frou, completely recovered now, was, for her, in excellent spirits and eager to talk. Mrs. Plushington also was less hysterical and less unattractive to look at than last time.

William Wilmer's chief difficulty lay in softening and expurgating Frou-Frou's remarks, for had he translated her "dear, dear thoughts" without change, he was sure Mrs. Plushington would have had another collapse. By considerable quick thinking he managed to make Frou-Frou's acid comments on Mrs. Plushington, her mental processes, and her household fairly acceptable. And he did discover many useful criticisms on her diet, hours of sleep, exercise and so on.

He also uncovered the fact that the secretary had slapped Frou-Frou *hard*, the day before yesterday; but he didn't tell Mrs. Plushington that either — he knew it would only mean a great deal of trouble for someone. He decided to speak about it to the secretary in private, but realized that even this was unnecessary when Frou-Frou, grinning wickedly, added: "I got even with him though. His best trousers, one silk sock and four stitches in his ankle — that's what that slap cost *him*."

When the hour was only half gone Frou-Frou went to sleep, which put a sudden end to the tête-à-tête. Mrs. Plushington, however, was delighted with the results of the first interview.

"Dear, *dear* Mr. Wilmer," she cried, "it is perfectly miraculous, I mean it *really* is. Already we have learned *so* much, our understanding is so *greatly* improved. Why I never *dreamed* that she disliked shrimp salad. And to *think* that I have deprived my darling of peach Melba, because that idiotic veterinary said it was bad for her. Oh my dear, *dear* Mr. Wilmer, I cannot *begin* to express my gratitude."

William Wilmer hoped she wouldn't try, and explained that he had taken the liberty of bringing Mr. Keeler along for the ride. He hoped she didn't mind.

"Not at all, my dear boy, not in the least. I'm simply *delighted*. Any time that you would care to use the car do *please* consider it at your disposal, Pierre has practically *nothing* to do. And by the way, he takes Frou-Frou out for her airing in the Park every afternoon from four to five. If you have some friend who would care for the ride it would be the *greatest* pleasure — "

"Thank you very much," said William Wilmer, "I think Mrs. Keeler, she's my landlady, would love to go sometime. She doesn't get out much."

"You dear, *thoughtful* lad," she cried, "Pierre shall call for her at four tomorrow. And now au revoir — until next Sunday."

The footman hastily tossed away his cigar as he sprang out to open the car door; Pierre touched his cap; and Mr. Keeler greeted him jovially: "Why, you're early Willie, thought it was to be an hour. I'm just getting acquainted with the boys. Peer, here, has two cousins living in Lynn, Mass. Won't the old lady get a kick out of that?"

"Why that's fine," he answered. "I'm sure she will."

"Home Peer," called Mr. Keeler, leaning back and knocking his cigar ashes into the silver ash-tray, "and don't spare the ethyl."

The next item in the engagement book was his luncheon with the Mayor at City Hall on Monday. William Wilmer had rather dreaded this occasion, for he feared considerable formality and worried about what to do with knives and forks and things, also about his conversational ability.

He could have saved himself all this, for lunch con-

sisted of just crackers and milk on the Mayor's desk and after a few minutes he realized that he needn't have worried about table manners at all: the Mayor didn't. He needn't have worried about conversing either, for the Mayor did all the talking.

He was introduced to Inspector Dolan, in charge of the Mounted Police. "You have no idea, Commissioner," said Inspector Dolan, cordially, "of what a difference your appointment has made already. Why you wouldn't know the Mounted Division, the officers and horses are getting on so fine together. It's a great gift you have."

William Wilmer smiled and said, "I'm afraid your men are a little nervous, Inspector. One of the horses tells me that the officers are all scared to death of the tales that may be told on them by their mounts. He even said that Inspector Dolan's horse had — I believe he said 'an earful' for me." The others present all laughed loudly at William Wilmer's one remark of the day.

When the luncheon was over the Mayor ordered a police car to take him back to the Zoo. He would have enjoyed the ride very much if they hadn't gone so fast. He was quite terrified at the way they dodged through traffic, passed red lights and swung around corners with the siren going full blast. "My goodness," he said to himself, "I thought Mr. Gallagher was reckless, but he's nothing to this."

As they drew up before the office in a shower of flying gravel the Police officer glanced at his watch and remarked, "Not so bad, eight minutes flat from City Hall."

"Think of that," said William Wilmer, limply sliding out of the car. "Thanks very much."

"Not at all, Commissioner," smiled the driver. "It's a great privilege. Hope I can drive you again sometime."

"*I* don't," murmured William Wilmer as he hastened toward the refuge of his quiet office.

Then there was his first radio appearance on the Peppermint Patooties Parade. Miss Sweeney had agreed (for a thousand dollars extra) that he would interview Toby during the three minutes, forty seconds allotted.

So, on the evening of the broadcast he, Toby and Mr. Gallagher all squeezed into a taxi and went down to the P. I. P. Studios. It was quite a squeeze too, for Toby insisted on sitting on the back seat with his head sticking out of the open top so that he could see the sights, which left very little room for anyone else.

They attracted quite a bit of attention going through the lobby of the P. I. P. Building, but at least William Wilmer was protected from the autograph hunters, all of whom gave them a wide berth. They also had the elevator to themselves, for none of the operators would enter the car with Toby, so Mr. Gallagher had to run it.

The broadcast itself was quite dull. The studio audience applauded loudly as William Wilmer and Toby entered and took their places before two microphones. Miss Sweeney and the Keelers, of course, were in the front row, accompanied by Director Carrington-Carr.

Toby really looked very handsome, for Keeper Gallagher had spent the whole afternoon combing and brushing him. He enjoyed the applause and smiled pleasantly, giving a slight yelp when he recognized the Director. Over the radio the yelp sounded like a motor car accident and made the Patooties Orchestra musicians even more nervous than they had been. They played an overture, somewhat quaveringly; then William Wilmer read a short speech. It had been written by the Blither Agency and didn't seem, to him, to make much sense. It apparently bored Toby too, for he suddenly yawned loudly, which brought a great laugh from the audience.

Then they were supposed to hold a conversation. This, of course, was a pure fake. While they made believe talk to each other the engineers behind the scenes played a transcribed record of Letty O'Gargle and Charlie McNasty's voices. Their remarks were very silly, but it all seemed very wonderful to the audience.

While this was going on William Wilmer and Toby really did converse, for no one could hear them.

"This is awfully tiresome," said Toby. "Let's go home."

"Oh, we can't go quite yet, Toby," William Wil-

mer answered. "We still have a minute and a half to go. You see I'm being paid six thousand dollars for this."

"Well, I'm not," Toby growled a bit sulkily. "And I haven't had even a sniff of a crooner yet, or one of those moaning girls."

The interview was finished now and an announcer approached the microphone. "Is he a crooner?" asked Toby eagerly, licking his chops.

"No, *no*, Toby," William Wilmer answered hastily. "He's just going to read the Patooties advertisement."

Toby voiced his disappointment with a roar. For Toby, it was quite a small roar, but for a broadcasting studio it was tremendous. The microphone flew

one way and the announcer flew another. The microphone landed on Toby's paw and the announcer landed in the bass drum. The microphone hurt, and Toby let out a really *loud* roar. This was too much for the musicians, who hastily fled, leaving their violins, trombones, chairs and music racks scattered about the stage. The announcer, who was stuck in the drum, stayed where he was.

"Oh, goodness, Toby, you shouldn't have done that!" cried William Wilmer.

"I'm sorry," said Toby rather sheepishly, "I guess I spoke out of turn." He helpfully straightened up two or three chairs, retrieved a bass viol from under the piano and said, "Well I guess we can go home now." The audience cheered, whistled and clapped, while William Wilmer held the microphone for the announcer, still stuck in the drum, to make the closing announcement.

They held quite a little reception in the lobby. Miss Sweeney, the Keelers and Director Carrington-Carr were all there to congratulate them. "Oh, Toby," cried Miss Sweeney, opening her eyes wide. "You were *won*-derful!" Toby purred proudly as she stroked his ears.

"William, tell your partner he gets an extra joint of beef tomorrow," laughed the Director. "He was magnificent; stole the whole show."

Mrs. Keeler extracted an orchid from the corsage that Miss Sweeney had given her for the occasion and stuck it in Toby's mane, just over his left ear. "There now, Pussy," she cried, "you're a real radio star — orchids and everything." Toby purred still louder and rubbed against Keeper Gallagher's legs so hard that he almost upset him.

Mr. Wentworth Pringle, President of the Peppermint Patooties Corporation, and Mr. Blither joined the group — not too closely.

"It was sensational, Wilmer," Mr. Blither exclaimed, "the most unique performance ever staged in the history of radio! Really revolutionary — I mean *really* revolutionary!"

"Thank you," said William Wilmer. "I'm sorry about that drum though, maybe next week we'd better feature a rabbit."

Mostly the days passed in peaceful and happy succession. William Wilmer completed his survey of all the animals in the Zoo and began the series of interviews for the *Post Companion*.

It was great fun doing these. Keeper Gallagher would bring out two camp chairs and while William Wilmer chatted with whatever animal had been selected, Miss Sweeney would jot down their remarks in shorthand as rapidly as he could repeat them. Then she would disappear into the office and the next time he came in, there on his desk would be the whole interview, all neatly typed and bound in a cover.

Lucy, of course, was the first subject, and was a most willing performer. She loved to talk and did so with such enthusiasm that Miss Sweeney's hand fairly danced as she jotted down the notes. Her talk was interesting though. She spoke of Burma and of her childhood in the jungle, of her first contact with men and her labor as a work elephant. She told her impressions of the long trip across the Pacific, of her seasickness and her cold, wet arrival in America. She told of her impressions of this country and its people. And she complained a great deal of her foot trouble.

When Director Carrington-Carr read this first interview he had said, quite seriously, "William, this is a great document; Charlie Pulpwood certainly is getting his money's worth. If the rest are as good as this one I wouldn't be at all surprised if you got a medal from the National Zoological Society, and you'd deserve it. There's never been anything like this — ever."

It was during Lucy's interview that Mr. Twitch had appeared. Miss Sweeney's pencil had been flying, William Wilmer had been translating rapidly, when he suddenly became aware of an old, familiar, rasping voice. "Why, hello, Wilmer," it was saying. "Quite a personage now, I see by the papers. The animals' pal and all that. *And* Miss Sweeney — well, well, a regular S. S. & C. Company Old Home Week."

For a moment the old familiar fear coldly gripped William Wilmer. Then he looked up at Mr. Twitch. He was astonished to see how insignificant, in the bright noonday sun, Mr. Twitch really was. To see how cheap and shoddy the double-breasted suit appeared, how gaudy the show handkerchief, and how pasty and unhealthy the man himself actually looked.

He realized that Mr. Twitch was still talking. "It

just occurred to me, Wilmer, that you really need a manager. A manager and financial adviser. Now you know that my many years of experience with the S. S. & C. Company really fit me — "

William Wilmer looked hard at Lucy.

"Lucy," he said quietly, in his animal voice, "there stands the meanest, most unpleasant man I have ever known."

"Well now, he certainly looks nasty," said Lucy, moving closer to the rails and tentatively reaching out her trunk, "and of all the horrid suits I've ever seen!" She sniffed softly at the back of Mr. Twitch's collar. "Well, what do you think we ought to do about it?"

"I wouldn't like to suggest anything," he said mildly, "but I was just sort of thinking. Now that pool of Ruth's — "

Ruth, the hippopotamus, lived next to Lucy, and her pool, though probably very delightful for hippopotami, could hardly be called sparkling or sanitary.

Skillfully Lucy slid her trunk under Mr. Twitch's collar, wrapped it around what he called his chest and lifted him, screeching and wriggling, high in the air. Slowly she walked over to the dividing rail, held him awhile over the odorous pool and then gently dropped him in, head down.

"Why Lucy," cried Ruth indignantly. "Of all things! I've gotten resigned to chewing gum and

banana peels and Heaven knows what, but this is *too* much!" She plunged into one end of the pool as Mr. Twitch scrambled out the other.

William Wilmer almost felt sorry for the bedraggled thing sputtering wrathfully in the gravel path. His wet hair revealed how bald he was becoming, the cocky little mustache now lay limp, and from under the double-breasted coat hung dripping shirt tails.

"Oh, Mr. Twitch," called Miss Sweeney sweetly, "your slip's showing."

Lucy raised her trunk high, trumpeting gleefully, and that was the last they ever saw of Mr. Twitch.

CHAPTER IX

Walter

‾‾‾‾‾‾‾‾‾ T ‾‾‾‾‾‾‾‾‾
HE DAYS drifted by
happily while William Wilmer completed his survey
of the Zoo's animals. The interview with Lucy had
been received with great enthusiasm by the *Post
Companion*, and now Mr. Bullington Livingston was
making the illustrations. She enjoyed posing very
much, but was somewhat disappointed that she
couldn't talk with him.

"It's a shame, Mr. Wilmer," she declared, "I'd just
love to learn something about art, but he can't talk a
word of Animal. And Mr. Wilmer, don't you think
he's made my nose a little too long?"

He explained to Mr. Livingston that Lucy was
quite sensitive about the length of her trunk so the
artist obligingly painted out several inches of it.

"Oh, that's ever so much better," she cried delightedly, "*ever* so much."

For the moment there was really very little for William Wilmer to do at the Zoo and he was glad when the Circus came to town. He had signed a contract to act as Animal Consultant to the Greater Tingaling Circus, so as soon as they arrived he went over to the Garden to interview the animals.

There were a great many of them and he was kept very busy for two days, although having just come from winter quarters they were all in fine health and spirits and had few complaints to make. There were the usual protests about their traveling accommodations, of draughts and so on, but nothing at all serious — except Walter.

Walter was the trained seal who played the cornet and was probably the greatest seal virtuoso in the world. However, right now he was being very difficult; Mr. Tingaling was greatly upset and the trainer was in despair.

"It's just that he's an artist, Mr. Wilmer," the trainer explained. "He is a very great artist and all artists are temperamental."

William Wilmer could see that the seal was in a highly nervous state, so he questioned him quietly in Animal.

"It's *true*, Mr. Wilmer," Walter cried, "I *am* temperamental and high-strung and I just can't *stand* these crowds! Crowds of people all staring at you, clapping and whistling and making noises. And this continual

traveling, everlastingly moving from one place to another. My nerves are just ragged, I can't sleep at night, I've lost my appetite. And my music is suffering; why, this morning at rehearsal I broke down twice in the middle of 'Cavalleria Rusticana.' It's terrible, Mr. Wilmer, it really is!

"And after all the advertising they've done! I'm just terrified that I'll disgrace my trainer, and he's been so kind and considerate — he's worked so hard with me. It was all right in winter quarters, where I had my own private room and pool and could practise quietly all day without any disturbance, but this is just impossible. I know I'll go to pieces! I just *know* I will."

He was quite hysterical now, so William Wilmer tried to encourage him as much as he could. "Oh, I'm sure you won't do that, Walter," he said soothingly. "You're too great an artist. Now why don't you try

to get a good nap and a rest? Have you tried aspirin?" But Walter just shook his head hopelessly.

"And I'll come and talk with you as often as I can," Mr. Wilmer went on. "It's some help to talk isn't it?"

"Yes indeed it is," replied the seal gratefully, "and I'm ever so much obliged to you. But I just don't know; I feel all fluttery inside."

William Wilmer advised that Walter be given as much privacy as possible and as they walked away said to Mr. Tingaling, "I'm afraid he's on the verge of a nervous breakdown."

"I am too," the circus owner said gloomily. "And it's a shame. We've spent a lot of money on Walter and advertised him all over the country. He certainly is a genius, but after all, a genius who can't stand the sight of an audience isn't much good to a circus."

Mr. Tingaling had presented William Wilmer with a box for the opening night, so he gave quite a party.

Director Carrington-Carr came, very distinguished in evening clothes, and Mr. and Mrs. Keeler, the lat-

ter fairly sprouting orchids. Miss Sweeney, and Keeper Gallagher with his wife and five of the seven children, made up the rest.

Everyone was in the jolliest of moods. Miss Sweeney, as excited as any of the Gallagher children, bought them balloons, crackerjack, popcorn, peanuts, lemonade and ice-cream cones. The youngest one sat in Mr. Carrington-Carr's lap all evening and insisted on sharing her chocolate ice cream cone with him. Most of it went on his beautiful white shirt bosom, but he didn't seem to mind at all.

William Wilmer had always loved circuses, but this one was unusually thrilling. Their box was right down on the ringside and in the Grand Parade and Spectacle all the horses and elephants, the donkeys, trained dogs, seals, zebras, camels and giraffes saluted as they passed by. Most of the trainers, the acrobats, the equestrians and clowns had become acquainted with William Wilmer in the past two days and they all waved too, while the very pretty trapeze artistes threw kisses — which were enthusiastically returned by Mr. Keeler. The bicycle-riding bear tried to greet them in the middle of his most intricate figure and almost suffered a bad fall, to the great delight of the audience.

Midway of the performance it came time for Walter's act. Everything else stopped and the lights were lowered as he took his place on a stage in the center of the arena. From the despairing glance that he had turned toward their box William Wilmer knew he was still very nervous. He could tell that the trainer was worried, too, from the way he fussed around with the music rack and fiddled with the silver cornet.

Walter did very well with his first piece, "The Star-spangled Banner." The audience stood up and sang it and applauded wildly when it was over. He got through "The Old Folks at Home" well too, but William Wilmer felt very nervous and sympathetic when he started on "Cavalleria Rusticana."

At about the fourth bar Walter struck a frightfully sour note. He bravely started again, but this time only played two or three bars before breaking down. For a moment he hesitated, then with a hopeless gesture dropped the cornet, flopped down from the stand and clumsily galloped across the arena straight to Wil-

liam Wilmer's box. Frantically he hauled himself over
the railing, scrambled into a chair between William
Wilmer and Mrs. Keeler and buried his face in his
flippers.

"Oh, Mr. Wilmer, I knew I couldn't do it," he
sobbed. "I *knew* I couldn't! Oh dear, I'm *so* ashamed."
Tears streamed from his great brown eyes.

Mrs. Keeler put an arm around him and drew him
close. "Why, the poor lamb," she cooed, "the poor,
dear lamb. Come to Mother." She stroked his soft
head gently, murmuring endearments and slowly the
sobs and tremblings ceased, his eyes closed, and
throughout the rest of the performance he slept quietly, his head pillowed among Mrs. Keeler's orchids.

Toward the end of the show Mr. Tingaling entered the box, carrying the beautiful silver cornet. "Well, Mr. Wilmer, I just don't know what we're going to do about Walter," he said sadly.

"*I* do," Mrs. Keeler spoke up. "We're taking him home with us, that's what we're going to do. There's a vacant room up on the third floor he can have, and a bathroom with a great big tub that he can swim in. He'll stay up there with no one disturbing him and play his horn from morn to night, won't you dearie?" Walter wiggled his whiskers slightly and continued to sleep.

Arrived home, the still slumbering virtuoso was carried up to the third floor by Mr. Keeler and gently placed on the bed. Mrs. Keeler filled the tub and laid the cornet on a chair, while William Wilmer, leaning over the bed, spoke softly, "There now, Walter, everything's all right. Get a good sleep and don't worry."

Walter opened one eye and murmured, "Oh, Mr. Wilmer, it's *so* quiet and peaceful here, I could sleep for a week. Thank you all for being so good to me."

"Keeler," said Mrs. Keeler, "there's two kippered herrings in the icebox. Run down and fetch them, the poor lamb may wake up hungry."

"Those are my breakfast kippers," he objected, but she interrupted, "Get the fish and don't stand there arguing. You'll have an egg — maybe."

Next morning William Wilmer was waked by the pleasant strains of distant music. He lay and listened as the clear and accurate notes of "Cavalleria Rusticana" floated down the stairs, with never a falter. Going up, he knocked gently and went in. Glistening from his bath, Walter sat in a chair, gazing out the window with an expression of supreme happiness. He hugged his silver cornet lovingly.

"Oh, Mr. Wilmer," he burst out, "did you hear it? Not a single mistake. It was just as *easy!*"

"Yes, it was beautiful," he answered.

"This is just the loveliest room," Walter rattled on joyously, "so quiet and peaceful! I haven't slept as well in months. And I've just had the most refreshing bath — I hope I didn't splash too much. And I hope the music didn't disturb anyone, I muted the trumpet."

"No, it was very pleasant to wake up to," William Wilmer answered. "Why don't you un-mute it and play 'Reveille'?" He opened the door and as Walter sent the clear lilting notes of "Reveille" echoing down the stair-well they both smiled to hear the sounds of the rest of the household rousing, highlighted by a tremendous yawn from Mr. Keeler's room.

"You might do that every morning," William Wilmer suggested.

"Yes indeed," agreed Walter, "and I could play 'Taps' every night. I do play 'Taps' beautifully, *I* think."

Walter soon lost his morbid desire for solitude. He did spend a great many hours in his room practising, bathing and napping, but more and more often he came flopping down the stairs to visit with Mrs. Keeler, whom he adored. He followed her around like an eager puppy as she went about her household tasks. He especially loved to sit in a kitchen chair and look on while she prepared dinner. He was always very good and never touched anything, but Mrs. Keeler spoiled him with endless tidbits and quite frequently Mr. Keeler had to have eggs for his breakfast, instead of kippers.

Many evenings he would bring his cornet down after dinner and play for them, sometimes classical music, sometimes old sentimental tunes, and one memorable evening he played Irish reels and dances. Keeper Gallagher and his wife were calling that evening and Mr. Keeler danced with Miss Sweeney and Keeper Gallagher danced with Mrs. Keeler. They

danced reels and jigs and square dances until the chandeliers rocked and Walter gasped for breath.

William Wilmer had never danced, but Mrs. Gallagher swept him up, showed him the steps, and before long he was stamping and swinging his partners as lustily as anyone. Never in his life had William Wilmer had fun like this and never in his life had he seen anything so fascinating as the way Miss Sweeney's mop of coppery hair swung about her face and shoulders when she whirled and spun, or heard anything so lovely as her gay ringing laughter.

Then, when everyone was quite exhausted, Walter played "Macushla," so beautifully that all the ladies cried and Mr. Keeler blew his nose very loudly indeed.

It was Walter, really, who started all the talk about a farm.

One morning at breakfast Mrs. Keeler said, "I just don't know what we're going to do about the poor lamb. Here it is getting warmer and warmer and if I open the windows the neighbors complain about his practising and if they're closed he'll roast up there. He needs sunshine too, and fresh air. I do wish we lived out in the country where he could have a brook or a pool to swim in and lie out in the sun on a rock and play his trumpet, with nothing to bother him except maybe the birds and the crickets."

"Me too," chimed in Mr. Keeler, "I'm no horn artist, but I certainly would like to get hold of a plow again. Remember the corn I raised up there on the old man's farm, before we was married — best corn in the County? And the cows we had? I used to milk twelve, morning and night."

At the Zoo, Lucy took up the same strain. "I don't know how much longer I can stand this city life, Mr. Wilmer," she complained. "Those streetcars and taxis racketing all night — I never sleep, and my feet are just killing me — and nothing to *do* but stand around in this stupid pen. I'm really a country girl, Mr. Wilmer, I'm used to *doing* something. Why in Burma I used to pull a plow or a harrow all day and *loved* it. I could plow a straighter furrow than any elephant in the herd. And as for clearing brush or carrying logs or stones, why I could clean up an acre in a day. And then there was always a nice cool pool or a brook to bathe in and squidge your feet — "

"That must have been very nice," said William Wilmer.

Later Director Carrington-Carr came lounging into the office, apparently with the same subject on his mind.

"William," he said, "you'll simply have to do something to get rid of all this money you're accumulating, it's disgraceful for anyone to have that much. You'll just have to buy a yacht or a country place or something. Do you enjoy yachting?"

"Oh, goodness no," said William Wilmer hastily. "At least I don't think I would. I took a trip over to Staten Island once on the ferryboat and I didn't feel at all well. No, I wouldn't like a yacht."

"Well then, it's a country place," laughed the Director.

"Everyone seems to be talking about a country place today," said William Wilmer, "Mr. and Mrs. Keeler and Walter and Lucy and now you. I'm perfectly willing — I'd love to have a farm; but gracious, they must be very expensive. I don't see how I could afford such a thing."

"Miss Sweeney," Mr. Carrington-Carr sighed, "just how much has our little pauper in the bank, as of today?"

Miss Sweeney looked at a slip on her desk and smiled: "Exactly eighty-seven thousand, four hun-

dred and sixty-nine dollars and fifty-three cents at
the moment. There's a check due today from the Patooties Corporation which will make it ninety-three
thousand, four hundred and ninety-six."

"And his income?" he asked.

"This year it ought to amount to about one hundred
and four thousand dollars," she answered, "unless
there are some new contracts; then, of course, it will
be more."

"Goodness gracious," gasped William Wilmer, "I
can't believe it."

"Now don't you feel that you can afford a farm,
just a little old cheap one?" laughed the Director.

"I guess I can," he admitted. "But then there are
so many other things. There would have to be some-
body to cook and someone to do the farming — I
don't know how to plow or milk cows or anything."

"That has all arranged itself," Miss Sweeney said
with a smile. "Mrs. Keeler is terribly anxious to live
in the country. She really has never liked the city very
much and, as you know, her boardinghouse has not
been a great success. In fact for years you have been
her only boarder, until I came, and Eleanor and
Walter.

"Of course Walter is part of the reason too," she
went on. "The neighbors have been complaining about
his practising and that third floor is awfully hot —
for a seal. So Mrs. Keeler would just be delighted

to go and cook and keep house and do every-- thing like that — if you decided to buy a country place.

"And then there's Mr. Keeler. You may not realize it, but he's an excellent farmer. He has talked to me a lot about it and showed me the ribbons he won at county fairs for all sorts of things. He really loves it, that's why he has never amounted to much here in the city."

"And there's Lucy," William Wilmer added excit- edly. "She keeps complaining about her feet and long- ing for a cool stream and a pool and soft grass. She says she loves to pull a plow too, and carry wood and move rocks."

"Excellent," cried Director Carrington-Carr. "Why, it's wonderful, you won't have to buy a trac- tor. Lucy is yours for the summer, William. It will do her no end of good. She *has* been very unhappy of late. Why, you'll have a regular rest farm for discon- tented animals!"

"It all sounds wonderful," said William Wilmer eagerly. "How do you buy a farm?"

"Good Heavens," said the Director wearily, " 'How do you buy a farm?' *You* tell him Miss Sweeney, I've got to look at my mail."

She explained to William Wilmer that first you had to decide where you wanted a farm, then what kind of farm you wanted. Then you read all the advertisements, saw real estate agents, looked at land and finally bought one.

"Oh dear," he said, "it all sounds terribly complicated. Won't you buy a farm for me, Miss Sweeney?"

"Of course," she said. "I'd love to. But next week, you know, you have to start on your tour of most of the zoos in the United States. Mr. Carrington-Carr has decided to go along with you — he needs a vacation — and right now I have to arrange your schedule, get your tickets and reservations, wire the Directors and all that. Why don't you run along now and tell Lucy that she's soon going to have a nice cool brook to squidge her feet in and that before long she can pull a plow to her heart's content?"

"Yes indeed," said William Wilmer. "I know she'll be happy about it. And thanks ever so much."

But Miss Sweeney was already buried in railroad schedules, directories and telegraph blanks and she hardly heard him.

CHAPTER X

Home Is the Sailor

THE NEXT DAY being Sunday, the Keeler living room became a sea of newspapers, as both the Keelers, William Wilmer and Miss Sweeney hunted through the Real Estate Sections of the Sunday papers. William Wilmer soon became completely confused by all the advertisements, but Miss Sweeney quietly wrote down neat lists of the possibilities, of dealers, telephone numbers and such things.

Mr. Keeler insisted that there must be so many acres of hay meadow, for Lucy would require a great deal of hay. There would also have to be so many acres for corn and a garden, and a barn large enough for Lucy and three cows. Everyone agreed on a brook and a small pond and Mrs. Keeler wanted a good big kitchen with lilacs outside the windows. William Wilmer didn't demand anything.

Miss Sweeney finally took all the lists up to her room to type, while Walter happily played "Home on the Range" on his silver cornet.

The next afternoon Miss Sweeney handed Director Carrington-Carr an envelope. "I think you had better take charge of this," she smiled. "These are: the schedule for your trip, your tickets, and your Pullman and hotel reservations. I think everything is correct — and your train leaves Pennsylvania Station at nine."

"You're wonderful, Miss Sweeney," said Mr. Carrington-Carr. "Now if you'll just see that our young friend catches the train, you will have three whole weeks to attend to that little matter of buying him a farm and making it fit for human — and animal — habitation. By the way, wouldn't my car come in handy? You're welcome to it. You drive, don't you?"

"Yes indeed," said Miss Sweeney. "It would be most useful, thanks lots."

Together with the Director, William Wilmer had paid a visit to Creeks's the week before and purchased, or rather accepted, a great many new clothes and several handsome traveling bags. Mrs. Keeler had packed everything and was now giving final instructions.

"Don't be leaving those beautiful pajamas and things all over the country now, Mr. Wilmer," she cautioned. "And do straighten out your hair a little before the photographers start taking pictures."

"And don't get your feet wet, Willie," laughed Mr. Keeler, "and don't take any plastic nickels — "

"Suppose *you* take those bags down to the taxi," his wife suggested ominously, "and stop being so sidesplitting. I'll certainly be glad when you can get a few rows of potatoes to talk to, they might appreciate your humor. I don't."

"Good-by," said Miss Sweeney, her nose wrinkling cheerily as she extended her hand. "Have a good time and don't worry, I'll take care of everything."

Walter, perched on the newel post, played "The Soldier's Farewell," and William Wilmer was off on his tour.

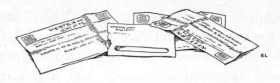

He had never traveled anywhere, except on the subway, so the trip, to him, was a tremendous thrill. The comforts and luxuries of the diners, the Pullmans and the hotels were amazing. The country they passed through, the cities they saw and the people they met were all new and wonderful to William Wilmer.

There was plenty of hard work, for visiting a new zoo every day or two and interviewing all its inmates was really quite a task; sometimes his small Animal voice became quite tired and hoarse. But all the Directors were so pleasant and so grateful for his aid that he enjoyed every moment. Most of them were rather like Mr. Carrington-Carr, jolly and easygoing. They had to attend many luncheons and some dinners, for everyone was eager to meet and see the famous William Wilmer. Frequently on these occasions he was called upon to make a short speech, but this was not difficult, for Miss Sweeney had written out a very nice one for him which he soon learned by heart. Everyone always complimented him on the interesting talk he had given and he always said, "Thank you very much," but he felt a little guilty about it.

In Atlanta, Georgia, on the fifth day of their tour, he was handed a telegram which said: —

HAVE FOUND LOVELY FARM MEETS ALL REQUIREMENTS SHALL I BUY

(Signed) MARY SWEENEY

"Goodness gracious, I never knew that," he said.

"Knew what?" asked Mr. Carrington-Carr.

"Her name is Mary," William Wilmer answered.

"You don't say so," said the Director patiently. (They were due at a Chamber of Commerce dinner in five minutes.) "Just who is it has such an unusual name, and is that all the information that telegram contains?"

"Miss Sweeney," he replied dreamily. "Her name is Mary" — and handed him the message.

The Director glanced through it and said: "Fine. Now please tie your necktie, or get a bellboy to do it, while I answer this; we're late already." William

Wilmer had his first evening clothes and always had considerable difficulty tying the bow.

So while he struggled with the tie, Mr. Carrington-Carr took a telegraph blank from the desk and wrote: —

OF COURSE
(*Signed*) WILLIAM WILMER

"There now William," he said, "you practically own a farm."

In New Orleans there was another telegram: —

DEAL CLOSED PLACE NEEDS A FEW REPAIRS SOME FURNISH-INGS AND DECORATING SHALL I GO AHEAD
(*Signed*) MARY SWEENEY

And William Wilmer answered:

OF COURSE DO EVERYTHING NECESSARY GIVE MY REGARDS TO WALTER

The next message came in Los Angeles, saying: —

MR. KEELER HAS LOCATED AN ELEPHANT HARNESS FOR PLOWING SHALL I BUY IT

And he replied: —

OF COURSE GIVE MY REGARDS TO MR. AND MRS. KEELER

In Seattle there was a letter containing several snap-shots. There was one of the house which looked very pleasant indeed. It was low and white and rambling. One wing seemed to be of stone but was mostly hidden by Mr. Keeler, who was posing coquettishly in the foreground. There were pictures of the barn and the brook and the pool, and there was one of Miss Sweeney sitting on the front steps. William Wilmer put this one in his wallet, but showed the rest to Mr. Carrington-Carr, who approved highly of everything.

The letter read: —

Dear Mr. Wilmer: —

Mrs. Keeler and I have been busy as bees, getting the house in shape. It is very old, built in 1785, and I know you will love it.

There is a wing that is perfect for the Keelers. Another wing, the stone one, has a big, comfortable study where you can do your work. I also bought the furniture, which is lovely. We have had some painting done and bought new curtains and a few rag rugs.

Mr. Keeler says that the barn is in excellent condition, that the land is very fertile and that he could raise enough hay for three elephants.

There is a brook, with a pool for Lucy, and there are lilacs outside the kitchen windows.

Mrs. Keeler has leased her boardinghouse to a niece from Brooklyn and is busy packing her things. Mr. Keeler thinks you ought to move out just as soon as possible after your return, for it is time to begin planting now. You would not know him, he is so filled with energy and ambition.

Please thank Mr. Carrington-Carr for the use of his car. We have driven out almost every day. Yesterday we took Walter and he just loved it. Ever since, he has been playing "My Little Grey Home in the West." It always makes Mrs. Keeler cry, but she is really very happy. Keeper Gallagher says that Lucy can hardly wait to get to the country and that Toby misses you — as we all do.

Sincerely yours,

MARY SWEENEY

It was the nicest and longest letter William Wilmer had ever received. He read it over a great many times, in fact at the Kiwanis Club luncheon in Denver he started to read it instead of his speech, causing quite a sensation.

They arrived home on a Thursday evening, just a little over three weeks from the date of their departure. William Wilmer was struck by the bare, cheerless look of the house, for Mrs. Keeler had packed all her favorite bits of china and pictures and sent them out to the farm. A great many trunks, boxes and bundles stood about.

"My goodness," he laughed, "you seem to be all ready to move."

"Yes," Mr. Keeler said. "We thought we'd ought to get out there as soon as we can. The garden really should have been planted before this and there's quite a bit of plowing to get done. The sooner the better, I guess." He spoke without much enthusiasm.

"We thought Saturday would be as good a day as any," said Mrs. Keeler, rather tonelessly. "My niece is coming from Brooklyn tomorrow to take over here, so we can go any time that suits you."

"Why, Saturday will be fine," said William Wilmer. He was considerably puzzled, for everyone seemed so gloomy, and he had expected them all to be excited and happy over the coming move. Even Miss Sweeney had had very little to say beyond telling him that the deeds and other papers concerning the farm were filed in his office.

Walter seemed the only cheery member of the household. He flopped around happily, but when he played "My Little Grey Home in the West," Mrs. Keeler burst into tears and Miss Sweeney went hastily up to her room. Abashed at the results of his music, Walter climbed disconsolately upstairs and went to bed without even playing "Taps."

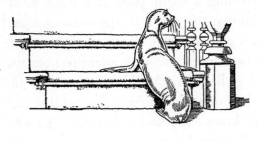

"Goodness gracious," said William Wilmer, "nobody seems very glad that I'm home — I don't quite understand it."

"There's a lot you don't understand," snapped Mrs. Keeler. It was the first time she had ever been cross with him and he decided that he might as well go to bed too.

His room had never been especially attractive, but tonight it was unusually desolate. Mrs. Keeler had packed all his belongings in an old trunk that now stood in the middle of the room. The curtains and bureau scarves were gone, the rug rolled up.

As William Wilmer sat desolately on the edge of his bed, his eye was caught by Aunt Edna's birthday card, still stuck in the mirror. It would be just six weeks Saturday since it had arrived. "My," he thought, "I never dreamed so much could happen in six weeks."

He looked around the little room that he had occupied for so many years and, dreary as it was, he couldn't help feeling a slight pang at leaving it. It occurred to him that this might be the cause of some of the evening's gloom. After all, this had been the Keelers' home for a long time, they might feel certain regrets at leaving. But why should Miss Sweeney be so silent? She had only been here a few weeks.

"I just don't know," he said unhappily, "I guess there *are* a lot of things I don't understand."

Next morning the atmosphere had not improved in the least. Miss Sweeney did not think she would go to the office, unless he needed her especially; there was a lot to be done around the house and she had promised to help Mrs. Keeler. Mrs. Keeler had little to say and Mr. Keeler just pulled his mustache and looked glum.

It was quite a relief to get away from the gloom of the Keeler home and greet Lucy at the Zoo. She was in great spirits, glad to see him back and bubbling with excitement at the prospect of the coming move. He showed her the photographs of the farm and she fairly squealed with delight over the meadows and the brook. "Oh, it's just *too* wonderful, Mr. Wilmer," she cried, "I can't wait to get there."

"Good gracious, Miss Lucy," he suddenly said, "I hadn't thought of it, but just how *are* you going to get there? I suppose we could get a big truck — "

"A *truck!*" interrupted Lucy indignantly. "Why Mr. Wilmer, am I a load of coal or something? A truck indeed! Why, I'm going to walk. It's all been arranged, I understand. Mr. Gallagher has found a howdah in one of the buildings here and he and that nice Mr. Keeler tried it on me yesterday. It's very becoming really, all red and gold. It will hold you and that lovely Miss Sweeney and Walter and his horn and your bags and my lunch — just a half-bale of hay."

"But isn't it too far to walk, Miss Lucy?" he inquired anxiously. "You've been having foot trouble, you know."

"Only eighteen or twenty miles, I hear," she said, "and gracious, Mr. Wilmer, that's just nothing. Why, I used to do thirty or forty miles in a day and think nothing of it. You've never seen me *really* walk, Mr. Wilmer. And as for that foot trouble, it's not half as bad as I've been pretending; the minute I get on some good soft grass I won't even think of it. But a *truck* — the very idea — I'd be so *humiliated!*"

Keeper Gallagher also was refreshingly cheerful. "Well, everything seems to be set, Mr. Wilmer," he said. "The howdah fits beautiful. Grogan will have Lucy over to the house at nine prompt, and I'll be there with the jalopy; the Director has give me the day off and I'll drive Mr. and Mrs. Keeler.

"Ought to be quite a parade," he chuckled, "I heard one of them Patooties fellers up here the other day talking with Miss Sweeney, and seems they're planning to have a float with banners and a loud speaker go along. The newsreel company's sending a sound truck and cameramen and of course there's always the reporters. The Police Commissioner himself was up yesterday with a permit and he's going to have two radio cars and two motorcycle cops to escort us. I only wish there was bagpipes, I love the pipers."

"Well, there's Walter and his cornet," William Wilmer smiled, "and the Patooties float. I guess we'll have plenty of music."

"Well, William," Mr. Carrington-Carr greeted him. "You're apparently moving in great style, gilded howdahs, sound trucks and everything. Sorry I can't join the procession, but I have to go up to Albany for the week end. Good luck though, and I hope you like the farm, I'm sure you will."

William spent the rest of the day puttering around the office and talking with the animals. Many of them had relatives in the zoos that he had just visited and he carefully delivered all the greetings and messages that had been entrusted to him. Toby seemed a bit disgruntled at the thought of his departure.

"Why, Toby," he said, "it's not very far and I'll be coming in every few days. And Mr. Carrington-

Carr has promised to bring you out some times for week ends. We can go woodchuck hunting; I used to do that on my uncle's farm when I was a boy; that ought to be fun."

"I guess it would," said Toby, brightening up somewhat. "Are there any crooners out there?"

William Wilmer felt much cheered up by his day, but at home that evening the gloom had thickened considerably. Mrs. Keeler's niece, whom she disliked intensely, had arrived from Brooklyn and that didn't help matters any. Miss Sweeney did not appear for dinner. "Headache," Mrs. Keeler explained shortly, "and no wonder, poor lamb." Which didn't explain anything at all.

Walter appeared timidly after dinner, but didn't bring his cornet, and discouraged by Mrs. Keeler's forbidding air soon flopped his way upstairs again.

William Wilmer vainly tried to interest someone by chatting about tomorrow's schedule and arrangements, but Mr. Keeler only continued to twist his mustache contemplatively, while his wife irritably opened and closed suitcases.

He finally gave up and announced, "Well, I guess we'd better turn in early. Tomorrow will be quite a day."

"It will indeed," Mrs. Keeler said, forebodingly.

CHAPTER XI

Lost and Found

WILLIAM WILMER had expected to rise early, but Mrs. Keeler had packed his alarm clock and it was after nine when he got downstairs. Outside he saw Lucy, very proud of the red and gold howdah strapped on her back. Mr. Keeler and Keeper Gallagher had placed a stepladder against her side and were busily loading bags and packages. Quite a crowd had gathered and the two radio cars were standing by.

Walter, very subdued, sat patiently on the living-room sofa holding his silver cornet and a small bucket of fish for his lunch. Mrs. Keeler was nowhere to be seen, but her niece gave him a hasty breakfast.

As he left the dining room he met Mrs. Keeler in the hall. She was carrying a basket of china and greeted him unsmilingly. "Well," she said, "we're about ready to go."

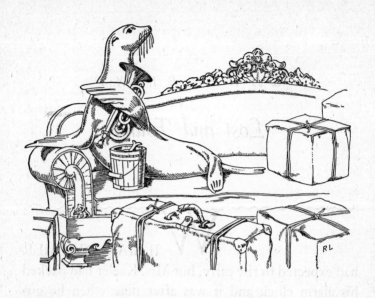

"That's fine," he answered. "I'll get my hat. Where is Miss Sweeney? I haven't seen her."

"You won't," Mrs. Keeler said shortly. "She's gone."

"Oh, gone on ahead, you mean? I don't blame her," he laughed. "Eighteen miles on an elephant is quite a ride."

"No — she hasn't gone on ahead, she's just — gone," Mrs. Keeler answered flatly.

Something in her tone and manner brought a chill empty feeling to William Wilmer. "Why Mrs. Keeler," he gasped, "what do you mean? You mean she isn't coming back — she isn't going — to the farm?"

Mrs. Keeler shook her head and sat down rather heavily in a chair.

The chill empty feeling mounted to panic. Not coming back! *Not going to the farm!* What did *he* want with a farm? What would he want with anything — his work, his fame, money, clothes? He choked at the thought of his lovely office — without *her*. Why, he would rather be back at the S. S. & C. office, in his shiny suit, punching the keys of his adding machine, but able to smile "Good morning" to her once each day, than face the desolate existence that Mrs. Keeler's "She's just — gone" threatened.

"Listen, Mr. Wilmer," Mrs. Keeler explained, "she's not coming back — and she's not going to the farm — she can't. Don't you ever read the papers? Haven't you seen Wally Wencher's column in the *Daily Bleat?*"

He remembered having occasionally glanced at Wally Wencher's gossip column, but the remarks were all so mean and low-minded, and so many of the people who were attacked unknown to him, that he had never paid much attention to it. He just shook his head with the stunned look of a kicked puppy.

Mrs. Keeler extracted a wad of clippings from her handbag and thrust them at him. "Well here, read these," she ordered.

William Wilmer glanced through them with unbelieving eyes, for they were all about him and Miss

Sweeney and they were all in Wally Wencher's most vicious style. His face burned, his head began to buzz, and he felt quite ill. He knew that for weeks the newspapers had been filled with articles about him, but he never dreamed that he had become prominent enough to fall a victim to Wally Wencher's malicious pen.

They were filled with phrases that burned in his mind like acid: "The gorgeous redhead . . . *supposed* to be his secretary . . ." "The little love nest in the Park . . ." "The Man Who Talks like a Monkey . . ." and dozens more in the same vein.

"The last one's the worst," said Mrs. Keeler grimly.

He read, half aloud: "We understand that the insurance-clerk Tarzan and his Titian-haired charmer have purchased a ducky little country home. No wedding bells, of course, but there's to be an elephant as chaperon, so everything's O.K."

"But — " he stammered — "what — why — I don't see — "

"Listen, Mr. Wilmer," Mrs. Keeler said, her patience stretched almost to the breaking point, "don't you understand that a nice young girl like Miss Sweeney can't be traipsing around with a rich and famous young gentleman like yourself without being talked about by nasty little rats like this Wally Wencher? And don't you understand that she can't be moving out to your lovely farm unless she's — unless you're — "

"Unless what?" he asked blankly.

"Good grief!" roared Mr. Keeler from the doorway. "Unless you're married!"

William Wilmer sat as though stunned. "But goodness gracious!" he finally gasped. "*She* — Miss Sweeney — marry *me*? Why, I wouldn't dare — I never dreamed — Mrs. Keeler, you don't *really* think she would possibly consider — "

"I don't *think* anything," she snapped. "But I can't help having eyes in my head and ears and a brain that works, unlike some people around here. And I know that when a nice sensible girl like her, the dear lamb, cries her eyes out for three nights steady, there's something more than a hair-do on her mind. And packs her bags and her books and her canary and goes off in a taxi at the screech of dawn, telling me she's got to get a new job and a new room and not telling me where she's going or her new address even — " She was snuffling now, mostly with irritation. From the sofa Walter moaned dolefully.

"And *you*," she rushed on, "*you* out talking to elephants and Mayors and crocodiles as big as life, and too dumb or too scared to say four decent words to a dear, gentle slip of a girl that's been looking after you like a mother and only getting herself gossiped about for her pains." She kicked the basket of china viciously and fixed a baleful eye on Mr. Keeler, who discreetly withdrew.

William Wilmer's experiences of the last few weeks — of meeting famous scientists, governors, mayors and admirals, of addressing banquets and luncheons — had given him much more confidence in himself; but the effect of Mrs. Keeler's revelation was amazing. The dawning of this great new hope burst on him like a blinding flash of sunlight, and in that flash a new William Wilmer was born. Gone were the timidity, the hesitation, the indecision. Gone was the William Wilmer of adding machines and Twitches.

He didn't have to think now what Director Carrington-Carr would do in such a situation, he *knew* what William Wilmer would do. Springing to his feet, he removed the Deputy Commissioner's badge from his vest, pinned it prominently on his coat and stepped quickly to the front door. A police lieutenant, lounging in one of the radio cars, leaped out hastily, ran up the steps and, saluting, said, "Yes, Commissioner, anything I can do?"

"Lots," William Wilmer said shortly. "Come in here. Now," he said when they were in the living room, "my secretary, Miss Mary Sweeney, is missing. I want her found at once — "

"Description?" asked the Lieutenant, whipping out a notebook.

"Height, five feet two, slender, weight about one hundred and ten. Red hair — " ("*Lovely* red hair," put in Mrs. Keeler.) "Eyes dark blue, black lashes.

Last seen was wearing — what was she wearing, Mrs. Keeler?"

"That sweet little blue linen jacket," she answered, through her snuffles, "a white linen skirt, flesh nylon stockings, black and white pumps — and no hat."

"Left this address," William Wilmer continued rapidly, "at 6:30 this morning in a taxi. Had three traveling bags, four cardboard cartons of books, a portable typewriter and a canary — " ("Name of Eleanor," added Mr. Keeler helpfully.)

"Thank you sir," said the Lieutenant, snapping his notebook shut. He went down the front steps two at a time, calling to the officer in the car, "Duffy, get Headquarters — Bureau of Missing Persons."

Within five minutes the teletype machines in every police station in the city and three adjacent states were clattering out the description of Mary Sweeney. In six minutes the occupants of every cruising police car in the five boroughs were eagerly scanning the side-

walks for a redheaded girl, five feet two inches, weight about one hundred and ten. Within ten minutes shrieking cars had carried details of officers and plainclothesmen to every railroad station, ferry, bus and air terminal. Three detectives, sent to the Safe, Sane and Colossal Insurance Corporation, gave Mr. Twitch a very terrifying fifteen minutes of questioning. Two others joyously hauled Wally Wencher from his silken-sheeted bed and subjected him to a not too pleasant cross-examination. Every taxi driver in the district was being questioned.

William Wilmer strode out to the car and gave the Lieutenant his snapshot of Miss Sweeney. "Fine," said the Lieutenant. "Duffy, call a motorcycle officer and send this down to Headquarters; have a thousand printed and sent out." Then, turning to William Wilmer: "Inspector Dolan of the Mounted Division is on his way up and the Commissioner himself will be here shortly. Anything else, sir?"

"You might get a few officers to take care of this crowd," he suggested. The Peppermint Patooties loud-speaker trailer, decorated with banners and a life-sized police horse, had arrived. The newsreel sound truck was waiting down the street and taxi-loads of reporters and photographers were constantly arriving.

He explained the delay to Lucy, who cried, "Why goodness gracious, Mr. Wilmer, how terrible! Now don't you give me a thought. I don't mind waiting here the least bit. Why I'll stand here for a week, I just won't move one step until that sweet girl is found! The very idea. I could do with a sip of water though."

So Keeper Gallagher brought her nine buckets of water and eased the straps which held the howdah, while William Wilmer paced the living room, Mrs. Keeler snuffled quietly and Mr. Keeler hauled at his mustache. Poor Walter, sitting patiently on the sofa, his sad brown eyes fixed on Mrs. Keeler, who hadn't even spoken to him all morning, tentatively fingered his cornet, sighed deeply and decided it was no time for music.

Inspector Dolan of the Mounted Division arrived, and was most sympathetic. "If you only had time to tell her description to the horses now, Commissioner," he said, "they'd be a real help — they're that sharp-eyed, and there's nothing they wouldn't do for you."

An hour or so dragged by. The Commissioner of Police himself came and assured William Wilmer that everything possible was being done, so far without much result. Four hundred and eighty-seven red-haired young ladies had been stopped and questioned, but none was Miss Sweeney. "I've told the Mayor the whole story," he said, "and he's ordered a Grand Jury Investigation of Wally Wencher, but that doesn't do us any good right now."

"*I'd* like to give him an investigation," growled Mr. Keeler. "If I could just get these two hands on that stringy neck of his I'd investigate him — inside and out."

Another half-hour passed, while William Wilmer continued to pace the floor. Every few minutes the Lieutenant appeared to report no success.

Then suddenly a last desperate hope inspired him. He rushed to the street, sprang into the jalopy and called Keeper Gallagher. "The Zoo," he ordered, "quickly."

Two motorcycle officers, their sirens wailing, swung in ahead of them and Keeper Gallagher made the Zoo in almost no minutes flat. They skidded to a stop in front of the Lion House; William Wilmer leaped out, dashed through the building and up to Toby's cage.

"Toby," he cried, "have *you* seen Miss Sweeney?"

"Certainly," yawned Toby, who had been taking a nap, "she was in here about half an hour ago. Seemed upset though — kissed me on the nose, and scratched my ears, and then went out the door there, toward the offices. What's the matter? Anything wrong?" But William Wilmer was gone. "Well, that's gratitude for you," Toby grumbled, and resumed his nap.

The office seemed even more peaceful and cozy than usual, as he burst in. Outside the bees hummed busily, the window curtains stirred gently in the soft spring breeze, the noise and rumble of the city seemed shut out and far away. There was a great bowl of flowers on the desk, and behind the desk, in his chair, sat Miss Sweeney. A neatly written note, which she had evidently just finished, lay on the blotter before her.

She looked up at William Wilmer's wind-blown hair, his disheveled clothes, his gold badge all awry.

"Oh, hello," she said.

Her calmness and the naturalness of the office almost wilted the courage which had sustained him all

morning. He began to blurt out a flood of explanation, of protestation and entreaty. In the midst of it he suddenly recollected Mrs. Keeler's bitter accusation, ". . . scared to say four decent words to a slip of a girl."

Straightening his shoulders and speaking as firmly as he had to the Lieutenant, he demanded, "Will you marry me?"

"Of course," she answered quietly, "if you really want me to." Her nose crinkled slightly. "When?"

His heart gave a great leap; for a moment dazzling flares seemed to burst before his eyes; then he resolutely gained control of his faculties.

"Right now," he said, glancing at his watch. "It's eleven-thirty and the License Bureau closes at twelve — and Lucy's been standing there since nine."

"Oh, the poor darling," she cried, springing up. She picked up the letter and tore it into small bits. "That was my resignation," she smiled, throwing the pieces into the fireplace, and then, "Oh dear, I'd forgotten Eleanor. He's at my new boarding place — and my bags, I must have *some* sort of trousseau — "

"Write out the address," he said, and when she had done so, grasped her hand and they ran for the car. He gave the slip of paper to one of the officers, saying, "Please ask the Lieutenant to send a car and get Miss Sweeney's bags and the canary — and oh, by the way," he added, "you might tell them Miss Sweeney's been found."

"I guessed that," he smiled — then saluted, and roared away.

As they clambered into the car William Wilmer called to the other officer, "City Hall — and we've only got twenty-five minutes."

"Twenty-five minutes," laughed the officer, grinning at Keeper Gallagher. "Why I could do it in twenty minutes — on roller skates. Stick behind me and if that wheelbarrow don't fall apart we'll do it in ten."

"Stick *behind* you!" jeered Keeper Gallagher, settling his cap firmly. "Just keep that kiddie-scooter out

of my path, or I'll be climbing up your fat back."
And as the motorcycle broke into a machine-gun roar
and shot off with a spurt of gravel, "Glory be," he
cried, "to think of having a cop ahead of you, instead
of behind you. This is going to be *a ride*."

It was *quite* a ride — a ride that Keeper Gallagher
recounted to his cronies for many a year. But William
Wilmer never remembered much of it. He remembered that the car was well loaded with Keeler baggage and that they were quite squeezed on the back
seat. He remembered the coppery glory of her wind-
tossed hair, her radiantly joyous smile. He remembered the warmth of her hand, clinging now to his
with the soft trustfulness of a little child's.

He remembered also a tearing sound as their car
left one mudguard draped around a fire hydrant and
Keeper Gallagher exuberantly calling over his shoulder, "We don't need it anyway, 'tisn't going to rain
today." He remembered Mrs. Keeler's iron skillet fall-
ing against his shin and being surprised that he felt no

pain. Once, after a particularly hair-raising series of swerves between and around several buses, Miss Sweeney called, "Oh, Mr. Gallagher, you're just *won*derful!" Keeper Gallagher, in his enthusiasm, attempted even more speed, but it was useless, for the accelerator had been down to the floor ever since they started.

As they whirled past one of the great jewelry shops on the Avenue William Wilmer cried: "Oh goodness, I forgot. Shouldn't there be a ring or something?"

She nodded, and with her disengaged hand extracted a gold band that hung from a thin chain around her neck. "It was Grandmother's," she called, "and Mother's. I've saved it a long time — for to-day."

Three additional motorcycle officers had joined their escort en route, and with a final blare of sirens the cavalcade swung into the City Hall Plaza. They slid to a stop just as the hands of the tower clock pointed to 11:50.

While the couple dashed up the marble steps, their original pacemaker drew up beside the jalopy, which was steaming now like a giant teakettle. "Not so bad Keeper," he laughed, "I didn't think she'd make it. Twelve minutes exactly from the Park."

"Twelve minutes!" responded Keeper Gallagher. "Shure that's disgraceful. If youse lads hadn't kept getting in me way we'd have made it in ten."

The Mayor, attracted by the sirens, had emerged from his office to greet them in the rotunda.

"Can you — will you marry us?" William Wilmer asked breathlessly. "Have we time to get a license?"

"One thing at a time," laughed the Mayor. "Do I get to kiss the bride?"

"I don't see why not," Miss Sweeney grinned. "I've already kissed a Nubian lion this morning."

He called to a secretary to have a license and a clerk sent over from the License Bureau at once and led them into the great Council Chamber.

"I'd always counted on having a church wedding," Miss Sweeney said, looking around the impressive old room, "but this certainly is next-best." She unclasped the ring from its little chain and gave it to William Wilmer.

"Put it right there on the table, in plain sight," the Mayor ordered. "You've already mislaid your bride this morning and I'm not going to start hunting around under furniture for any ring — not at my age."

While they waited for the license Miss Sweeney brought some order to her hair and Keeper Gallagher

and the motorcycle officer were summoned to act as witnesses. They were a bit wind-blown and dusty, but their uniforms gave quite a military air to the wedding party.

"You might have left off that big gun," grumbled Mr. Gallagher, in an undertone. "It makes me nervous, and it's *very* out of place." But the officer scorned a reply.

In a matter of minutes the license arrived, was filled out — and suddenly the Mayor, with great solemnity, was reading the service.

William Wilmer said "Yes" a few times and managed to get the ring on without dropping it; Miss Sweeney said "Yes" and Keeper Gallagher even added a few "yeses" of his own. Then everyone was shaking hands with everyone else and the Mayor was demanding, "My fee, Madame."

"Why Mr. Mayor," she cried, her deep eyes just a trifle moist, "you were just *won*derful!" and kissed him sweetly.

At that moment the bell in the clock tower boomed out the hour of noon, church chimes and factory whistles took up the chorus. "Come on, Pop," said the policeman, giving Mr. Gallagher a shove, "and get that sweet chariot swinging. I'm just dying to heave some rice at you."

There was a great popping of flashlights as they emerged from the City Hall, for word of the wedding had gotten around and the newsmen had gathered like flies.

"We needn't go *quite* so fast now, Mr. Gallagher," the bride said, as they wedged themselves into the rear seat.

"O.K.," he smiled, "Mrs. Wilmer."

"Goodness gracious," gasped William Wilmer in a dazed voice. "*Mrs. Wilmer* — think of that!" The iron skillet crashed down on his other shin, and again he felt no pain.

The good news had evidently preceded them, for when they pulled up before the boardinghouse Mrs. Keeler, arms outstretched, flew down the steps; Mary flung herself into them and they both wept joyously.

Mr. Keeler pumped William Wilmer's hand, Keeper Gallagher's hand and the Policeman's hand, cleared his throat raucously and threatened to pull his mustache from its roots.

Walter, barking happily, struggled down the steps carrying his cornet and his bucket of fish, now half empty. He skillfully negotiated the stepladder, and ensconced himself in the very front of the howdah. Lucy snatched up the last wisp of her luncheon hay, flapped her ears and trumpeted shrilly. Mary climbed nimbly up to her place; William Wilmer, less nimbly, followed her; the ladder was removed. The Keelers wedged themselves into the jalopy.

And now the radio cars sounded their sirens, the motorcycles roared into action, the Patooties loudspeaker blared forth, the neighbors cheered and deluged everyone with rice, Eleanor trilled ecstatically, and over it all, clear and sweet, the silvery notes of Walter's cornet burst into the Wedding March.

CHAPTER XII

Journey to Arcady

~~~~~~~~~~~~~~~~~~~~~~~~~~~~~

AT FIRST the going
was slow, for the streets were crowded with week-
end traffic and everyone wanted to get a look at the
wedding party. However, when they reached the
Parkway, the sound trucks and the Patooties trailer
were turned back, Lucy took to the grass shoulders
and their speed increased.

"My goodness, Mr. Wilmer," she called happily,
"but it's delightful to feel real grass under your feet
again! Didn't I tell you I could *really* walk; just you
wait until I get limbered up and I'll show you what
speed is."

Mrs. Keeler had packed them a basket of lunch
which was now opened. William Wilmer was too
excited to eat much, but Mary devoured her share

and part of his with great relish. "I didn't have any breakfast," she confessed, "I was too busy packing — and running away."

"Don't mention that," he shuddered, "it was too awful."

"I won't," she promised, "I'll never mention it or think of it again — ever. It wasn't pleasant."

Walter finished his fish, yawned happily, and leaned out to wave at the Keelers who had drawn up alongside. Mrs. Keeler called that they were going on ahead to start dinner, Keeper Gallagher stepped on the gas, and amid derisive toots of the Policeman's siren they clattered off up the road.

"Officer," William Wilmer called down, "I don't think we'll really need you any more. Could you do anything with half a cold chicken and some ham and stuff?" He slipped a good-sized banknote into the basket and lowered it down. "Thanks a lot."

"Thank *you*, Commissioner," beamed the Policeman. "I'll just polish this off and then I'll be getting back and report to the Inspector and His Honor that the honeymoon's off to a *swell* start. Good luck to you and the lady." He drew off to the side of the road, Lucy resumed her progress and as they rounded the next curve Mary threw a kiss, to which he responded with a gallantly flourished drumstick.

Lucy's strides grew steadily longer until her fast, steady walk was almost a lope, that never varied or slackened. William Wilmer was astonished by the speed with which she could cover ground. The sun was warm and the howdah had a pleasant rolling motion that was most restful, once they were used to it. Eleanor twittered softly in his covered cage. Walter, after several yawns, stretched out with his head in Mary's lap, gave a contented grunt and went to sleep.

She said drowsily, "Our road turns off about five miles from here. It's called the Blue Valley Road — you can't miss it — but you'd better tell Lucy — in — case — you . . . go . . . to . . . sleep . . . too. . . ." Her voice trailed off, her head, pillowed in glowing hair, rested on William Wilmer's shoulder and she also slumbered.

He called softly to Lucy to tell her about their road. "That's all right Mr. Wilmer," she said, "I'll see it, don't you worry a bit. Why don't you take a nap too, you've had quite a day?"

"Oh, I don't feel the least bit sleepy," he laughed. "I'm too excited and happy. Don't hurry *too* much, Miss Lucy," he added — for she was breathing rather heavily, by now. "You haven't had much exercise for a long time, you know."

"Oh this is *nothing*, Mr. Wilmer," she called. "I *am* a little out of condition, my wind isn't what it used to be; but it doesn't bother me, and my feet feel just fine. Besides, I'm *so* anxious to see the farm — and I'm sure you are, aren't you Mr. Wilmer?"

"Yes indeed," he answered happily.

They had long left the outskirts of the city behind and were now passing through beautiful rolling farm country. White houses nestled among thick clumps of trees, some of the fields lay brown from fresh plowing, others were dazzling with the young green of newly sprouted crops. In pastures, black and white

and red cows gazed in wonderment, and many broke into awkward flight at the sight of Lucy's swiftly moving bulk surmounted by the rocking red-and-gold howdah.

With every mile William Wilmer's spirits rose to greater heights of happiness. The sick despair of the morning, the lost, desolate hopelessness, seemed years away. A wisp of the glorious red hair, tickling his left ear, a soft regular breathing, were assurance that his ecstasy was real and not a dream.

Lucy's voice burst into his thoughts — "This is it, isn't it, Mr. Wilmer?" — as without any slackening of speed she swung into the Blue Valley Road. It was a real country road, shaded here and there by arching elms, cross-striped with shadows by the late afternoon sun. The roadside grass here was deep and lush; Lucy occasionally swept up a trunkful and tossed it into her mouth without the slightest break of her swinging stride.

Mary stirred, then came awake and pushed the disordered mop of hair from her face. "It's funny," she said, "I knew we had left the Parkway, I knew we were nearing home. The second road on the right is *our* road."

She lifted the cloth to inspect Eleanor, made a few pats at her clothes and laughed. "My. I hadn't realized that elephant riding was so dusty, we'll all want baths, especially poor Lucy — isn't she marvelous?

Why Lucy," she called, "you're just *won*derful!"

Lucy couldn't understand the words, but she recognized the voice and sensing the admiration flapped her ears and increased her pace. Walter too, waked up, yawned, looked around happily and moved up to the front of the howdah. He clapped his flippers together, picked up his cornet and sent peal after peal of silvery notes ringing across the quiet countryside. He played "The Light Cavalry Overture," and "A-Hunting We Will Go" and "The Caissons Go Rolling Along" in double time.

"That's just lovely Walter," Lucy puffed, "there's nothing like music to lift your feet," and lengthened her stride still more.

Mary was wide awake now, her eyes sparkled as excitedly as William Wilmer's; the mass of her hair blew back with the speed of their progress. "Here's our road," she called suddenly. "Tell her — quickly." He called, just in time, and Lucy took the corner like a speedboat rounding a buoy.

Theirs was a dirt road and Lucy squealed with delight as she felt its softness. Her great flat feet squelched out fountains of dust that surrounded them in such clouds that Walter had a sneezing fit and had to give up his musical efforts.

They were going up a slight rise, and as they approached the crest Mary's eyes grew wide as a child's on Christmas morning. She clutched his hand tightly

and breathed, "It's coming now!" As they reached the brow, Lucy, with sure animal instinct, slowed down and came to a momentary halt, sniffing with outstretched trunk the smell of *Home*.

William Wilmer held his breath. Below them the setting sun flooded the valley with a light that seemed almost a golden mist. In a slight hollow lay a broad stone and white shingled house, sheltered by towering elms and maples, their dark shadows striping across emerald green lawns. Up behind the house a great red barn reared its bulk like a protecting medieval fortress.

They saw details: a thin column of blue smoke rising from one of the many chimneys, the meandering course of a willow-shaded brook, the gleam of a pond, a purple-blue fog of lilacs by the kitchen, a tall slender pear tree clad in white blossoms. They saw the weary jalopy being unloaded by Keeper Gallagher and a shirt-sleeved Mr. Keeler.

Then, with a shrill trumpeting Lucy galloped wildly down the slope. Walter, as well as he could, blared a fanfare, the howdah rocked like a small boat in a

storm-tossed sea. Suitcases, lunch baskets, and Eleanor's cage tossed about their ankles. They thundered over a wooden bridge, swirled into the drive and came to a panting halt on the green lawn.

With a deep sigh and heaving sides, Lucy knelt down and they stiffly descended from the howdah, as Mrs. Keeler rushed out from the kitchen. Mr. Keeler and Keeper Gallagher hastened down to unload the bags, but Walter, who had spied the large wooden tank that had been built for him up near the barn, needed no assistance. With a glad bark he threw his cornet out on the grass, flopped over the side and went galloping up the grassy slope.

Eager to show her treasures Mary grasped William Wilmer's hand and rushed him toward the house, but they were halted by an outcry from the others.

"Carry her over the doorstep," Mrs. Keeler insisted.

So he did, but quite awkwardly, for despite her slimness she proved a difficult weight for his long-unused muscles.

"Wait till you've had a couple of months in the garden," roared Mr. Keeler, "with me as overseer, and you'll be tossing the old lady herself around like a bag of popcorn." He dodged a dish clout affectionately hurled by his wife and hastened back to the baggage handling.

They made a tour of the house, but William Wilmer was by now so dazed with it all that he could hardly take in the details. He didn't know much about architecture, or antiques, or old china or glass, anyway. But he did like the look of the dark oak floors, rich with the gleam of years of waxing, the sheen of mahogany and maple and walnut furniture, the immaculate ruffled curtains, the winking lights of brass and pewter. He could sense the comfort of the broad fireplaces, of the deep-set windows and the great stuffed sofas and chairs in his study.

Mrs. Keeler insisted that he admire the broad, low-ceilinged kitchen, her own domain — all its shining modern conveniences, the huge range, now simmering with dinner viands — and the lilacs outside the windows.

Mr. Keeler was clamoring for his approval of the outer premises, so they went out and he had the wonders of the barn explained; the quarters for three cows, soon to be bought, Lucy's stall, which had been made by combining three box stalls, the huge hay-mow, Lucy's new plowing harness, the corncrib, the chicken yard, the pigsty, the springhouse, all of them swept and whitewashed and scrubbed to a degree that gave him an entirely new respect for Mr. Keeler's capabilities.

"Goodness gracious," he said, as they walked back to the house, "this isn't — this can't all be — ours?"

"Every scrap of it," she smiled. "Every stick and stone and blade of grass — and me. And there isn't even a mortgage. Come now — I want to show you my favorite view."

They stood at the top of the pasture looking down over the whole farm. The sun had set but the golden light still lingered. Dimly they could see Lucy's huge bulk wallowing and splashing in the pool, in the still air her grunts and squeals of satisfaction carried clearly up the hill. They saw Mr. Keeler still busy-ing around the barn and the blue smoke of Keeper Gallagher's pipe. They saw the warm light of candles glinting on silver and china in the dining room. They saw Walter, sleek and shining after his swim, cavort-ing about the kitchen porch, saw Mrs. Keeler come out to shake her apron and stop to play with him.

Mary looked carefully at William Wilmer. Weeks in the sunshine interviewing animals had browned away the pallor of those years of servitude in the Safe, Sane and Colossal office. His hair, which used always to be limp and meekly parted, seemed to have thickened, it was alive and almost curly now. His shoulders, which had been getting a little rounded, were now broader, his back erect.

Lucy reluctantly heaved herself out of the pool, shook thoroughly and, raising her trunk high, trumpeted her contentment. Then she eagerly trotted toward the barn and supper. From the kitchen porch they caught the silvery glint of Walter's cornet and a moment later the lilting notes of Mess Call floated up the slope.

The very short nose, slightly sunburned now, crinkled ever so entrancingly, the black-lashed eyes widened and their blue deepened until it matched the evening sky.

"Oh William," she breathed, for the very first time, "you're just *won*derful."

"Thank you," said William Wilmer. "Thank you very much."